LOVE ME, DADDY

ELOUISE EAST

CONTENTS

LOVE ME, DADDY

CHAPTER ONE

NATHAN

Nathan Sanderson strode down the street, hands fisted deep in his bomber jacket as he headed for his usual destination. He was glad for the thick coat that kept the chill from sinking into his bones, although he wished he had something to stop it from freezing his nostrils. Focusing on the positive, he scented the freshness of the air; spring had arrived.

He veered left down an alley, cutting between businesses and homes to reach the exit on the other end. Glancing left and right, he crossed the road, avoiding the potholes which were more extensive the closer he came to his target. This run-down area of Cambridge was not the most lucrative for some people, but, it provided much-needed resources for him. Entering another alley, he slowed his steps, unzipped his jacket despite the weather and added a sway to his walk.

This alley was busier than others, and he nodded to several men he knew as acquaintances before switching his gaze to the other types of men. The buyers. Running his gaze over several of them, he chose the most likely of them: a guy with a balding head who was hunched into his padded winter coat and glancing furtively around.

"Hello, handsome." Nathan stepped closer to the guy, running a finger down the front of his coat with a coy smile on his face. "What can I do for *you*?"

"Um…oh…a…I want a blowjob." Apart from the initial stumbling, the words were exhaled in a rush, and the guy's onion breath bathed Nathan in eye-watering fumes.

Fucker must have just eaten. Inwardly, Nathan gritted his teeth and rolled his eyes. Outwardly, he pursed his lips and leaned closer to the guy's ear. "Would you like me to help with that?" He made sure to blow gently across the guy's ear as he spoke, providing stimulus to an already eager countenance.

The guy said nothing but bobbed his head vigorously.

Nathan leered at him, tugging gently on his coat as he stepped back towards *his* space. When he reached a six-foot gap between two wheelie bins, he paused, stepping closer once more.

"It's twenty for a blowjob. You okay with that?" Nathan never sold himself short, regardless of the degrading aspect of the position. The guy nodded once. "Shall I get down to business?"

The guy nodded once more and fumbled for the

money, pressing it into Nathan's hand. Nathan blew him a kiss and sank to his knees, making sure they were on the softer cushion of folded cardboard boxes instead of the bare ground. He didn't want any more stains on his clothes; he'd learned the hard way the first time.

Nathan tucked the money into his pocket and ran his hands up the guy's legs, feeling the tell-tale tremble of either nerves or excitement. Or both. He hoped the guy managed to finish and didn't let his nerves take over, leading him to run. He could do without having to find another source of income today.

Reaching for the guy's button, Nathan popped it open and unzipped, finding the cock behind held back by briefs. A slightly stale smell greeted Nathan, and he twitched his nose in response, lifting his gaze to the guy's face. The balding guy had his eyes tightly shut, sweat dotting his brow and his mouth wide open, panting as though he had run a mile. And that was before anything had happened.

Running his palm up the underside of the guy's cock, he felt the trembling increase and knew the guy wasn't going to last long. He pulled the briefs down, revealing a nice-sized dick with a slight curve in it.

Nathan wrapped his hand around the guy's shaft, fingers meeting, but only just. He stroked the guy a couple of times to get him used to the feeling and leaned forward to lick at the tip. The guy groaned emphatically; Nathan was sure the guy would blow his load before he had a chance to do anymore, but the guy managed to hold on. Not wanting to disappoint and potentially have the money taken back, he sucked the cock into his mouth, making sure to take him as far back as possible.

The guy thrust his hips and moaned. Nathan lifted his gaze and watched the guy's head drop back, and his hands clench by his sides. He was grateful the guy didn't fist his hair. Feeling restrained wasn't Nathan's favourite scenario. Now, give him a Daddy who took control over his life and cared for him, and Nathan would be more than content.

Concentrating he pressed his tongue on the underside nerves on every lift, Nathan put his all into the task. The guy's trembling increased tenfold, then he shouted and curled in on himself, thrusting his hips sporadically into Nathan's mouth.

Pulling back, Nathan wiped his mouth, shooting another coy glance up at his client. "Was it okay for you, handsome?" He ached for a favourable response; good results created return customers.

"Perfect." The guy began buttoning his trousers quickly.

"You know where I am should you need more relief, alright?"

The guy dipped his head, turned and shuffled away. Nathan rose and dusted off his knees, double-checking the money was still in his pocket. He sauntered out of his space, a sway on his hips as he left the alley. He had to keep in character as much as he could. It was the only way to get and retain clients.

As soon as he turned the corner, he sagged against the wall, exhaling loudly. As most homeless people did,

Nathan wished his life hadn't come to this. His *work* was a necessary evil. Getting food on the table—or rather on his lap—was more important than his dignity.

Inhaling a deep breath, he pushed away from the wall and hustled down the street towards the supermarket. Entering the shop was one of Nathan's favourite moments of all: the smell of fresh bread and fruit, the feeling of being anonymous amongst everyone else, the sounds of normalcy. All the aspects of an ordinary life that Nathan craved.

He picked up a basket and, knowing he had twenty pounds to spend, chose his food wisely. He grabbed a couple of tins of fruit, a loaf of bread, a jar of jam, a block of cheese, some crisps, a bottle of squash and some chocolate bars, and, as a treat, chose two small cartons of custard and three bananas, mentally calculating the cost as he went.

Bagging his items, he pocketed the change, which would allow him some leeway if he needed anything else over the next day or two.

The afternoon got darker, and Nathan hurried to reach his destination before the rain fell; there was nothing worse than sleeping in wet clothes.

Ducking down yet another alley, he squeezed his way through a hole in a wire fence and skirted the edge of the boundary line until he reached a small shack. Nathan glanced around to make sure there were no witnesses and knocked twice, opening the door and shutting it quickly behind him.

"There he is." Robbie was a bit younger than he

was, as was Daisy, but they all got along well enough to squat in the shack together. Each took turns in bringing something to the group. Last night, Robbie managed to get a blanket for each of them, which was an amazing feat. "Everything okay?"

Nathan nodded at the blond-haired man and threw a wink at Daisy. "Yep. I got us a little treat for later."

Daisy sat upright, her fingerless-gloved hands meeting with a muted double clap. "What is it?"

"Ah, ah, ah. That would be telling. I got some things for sandwiches. We should be able to keep most of it fairly fresh for a few days." Nathan grinned as he crouched on his side of the small torchlit area. He rustled through the carrier bag and produced the sandwich items, hiding the custard and bananas for later that evening.

Lowering himself to sit on his pillow—another remarkable find one evening—Nathan rested his head back against the cold brick wall and watched Robbie and Daisy make a sandwich each. He hadn't recovered from his *work*. He would eat a little later, but he reached for the water they had and opened the squash; the water had a metallic taste, which the squash overrode. Taking a deep drink, Nathan felt his body relax. He knew he had no other option, but it left a bitter taste—pun intended—in his mouth. He wished he'd bought a toothbrush and toothpaste because he didn't want to tarnish his meal with this horrid taste in his mouth.

One day, he would see a better way out of the position he was currently in. One day, he would be able to use his brain to earn money instead of his body. One day, he would have what Robbie and Daisy had. He flicked his gaze over to the lovebirds, currently snuggled underneath their blankets, wrapped around each other, talking quietly and kissing. One day.

CHAPTER TWO

LOREN

S itting in the café, sipping his lukewarm coffee, the lull of the conversations going on around him comforting rather than annoying, Loren Moore checked over the figures he'd input into the spreadsheet, saving the document. He clicked on his next project as someone dropped into the seat opposite him.

"It would be a miracle if Karen could get herself ready in time to be here." Ben grinned, rubbing a hand over his rugged, lined face.

Loren raised an eyebrow. "Well, if you waited for your wife instead of telling her to make her own way here, you would both be here."

Loren rolled his eyes at his two best friends. Ben and Karen had been married for fifteen years, and Loren was sure they would be married forever. Sometimes, he prayed for Ben's life, because every time he left his wife behind when she took too long to get ready, she threatened him with divorce, and Ben ended up sleeping on his sofa for the night. And Loren could do without it. Especially that night.

"Nah, she doesn't mind." Ben threw a wink at him and diverted his gaze outside to the car park. Loren knew he was scanning for his wife despite what he said. Ben had no patience whatsoever, but he loved the woman with every fibre of his being.

"That's not what my sofa says," Loren deadpanned.

Ben glared at him and returned his gaze to the view. "Anyway, how are things? Any luck finding your kink partner?"

"Ben!" Loren hissed at him, checking around them for people being close enough to have heard.

"What? You're looking, aren't you?"

"Yes, but I'm not advertising it to the whole city. Jesus, Ben." Loren picked up his now cold coffee, grimacing as he swallowed the remainder, hoping for another hit of caffeine.

"Well…" Ben shrugged, brushing off the fact that Loren tried to keep his Daddy issues quiet. "And you never answered my question."

He sighed. "No, I've not had any luck yet." He tried to keep his voice from sounding as melancholic as he felt. Finding a boy when Loren hated socialising was not an easy feat. He'd tried, time and again, the clubs catering for his type of kink, to no avail. Any other members he found with the same needs were either already attached or searching for boys, same as he was.

Loren could get his rocks off as well as the next

male, but it was always a disappointment when he realised he couldn't do *everything* he wanted to: tucking his boy into bed, caring for him, cooking for him, being what his boy needed as much as his boy being what he needed.

His last boy had lasted less than a year. Evan had told him he needed something less controlling and less twenty-four-seven, which was a bit of a shock when that was what they had agreed upon at the beginning of their relationship. Loren understood tastes could change, but it had thrown him when Evan had done a one-eighty about his requirements. Everyone is entitled to change their minds.

Even if it had made Loren camera shy now.

"You need to go further afield. I know—" Ben's words were cut off.

"I hope you're looking to have company tonight, Loren, because this asshole is pissing me right off." Karen's voice penetrated Loren's thought process, and he quickly switched his gaze to see her storming towards their table.

"Karen, sweetheart, you know how antsy I get when we're going to be late. I needed to get here, honey. You look beautiful, by the way, my sweet."

Karen slapped at Ben's shoulder when he tried to reach for her. "Don't you 'my sweet' me, you shithead. For once, I would love for you to consider that I want to arrive at the same time as you, not chasing after your coattails. When are you going to learn?"

Loren watched as Ben grabbed her and planted a kiss on her lips, witnessing Karen pretty much swoon into him. Ben pulled back, and Karen followed, blinking rapidly. Guiding her into the seat, Ben wrapped his arm around her shoulders with a smirk on his face directed at Loren.

That smirk meant Ben had won this round. Chuckling and shaking his head, Loren switched off his laptop and packed everything away.

"You're not heading home already, are you?" Karen's soft, melodic tone always calmed him for some reason.

"Yes. I need to get a few things sorted for the next lot of work I have arriving. I've recently taken on a few new clients, so I need to get them all set up properly before I can start them off." Loren exhaled wearily, his gaze focused on his packing. If only he had someone to relax with at home. Instead, he headed towards an empty, silent house. Maybe he should go out tonight and find someone to help him take the edge off.

Loren shook his head. No, it wouldn't work. He knew exactly what he needed, and he could find it nowhere around here.

"See you soon, you two." Loren dragged his coat on, shouldered his laptop bag and leaned down to kiss Karen on the cheek before striding to the exit. He didn't want to be accompanied tonight. He would bring the others' jubilant mood down.

Buttoning his coat as high as it would go and lifting the collar to cover his neck, Loren drifted towards home. Despite his assurances to his friends, he had nothing waiting for him, not even work.

By the time he'd made the twenty-minute walk,

Loren had lost the feeling in his fingers. His gloves had been misplaced at some point in the last week, and he had yet to replace them. He struggled to unlock his front door, and, once he'd entered, struggled to lock it again.

He pivoted but stayed frozen in the hallway, surveying his home. It was in a prestigious area, not extremely wealthy, but not bad either. He had bought it when property prices were low and had reaped the benefits of the choice now the market had risen. His bedroom was to the left off the main hallway, and he headed there first to drop off his laptop and paperwork; he'd sort everything out later.

Returning to the hallway, he removed his coat and shoes and trailed to the kitchen. More coffee was needed. It was only five-fifteen, but Loren felt like he'd been awake for days.

As the drink brewed, Loren thought back to Ben's words: he needed to go further afield. It wouldn't hurt, but Loren wasn't sure he had the energy. Not tonight, anyway. He was too tired of the emotional toll it took.

Taking his doctored coffee to the sofa, he sat, sipping the brew, waiting for the heat to warm his bones. He wrapped both hands around his mug as he sat in the corner and tucked his legs up underneath him. Staring at the blank TV, he tried to figure out what he was doing wrong. There must be something about him different from the other Daddies around; otherwise, one of the boys would have stayed.

Evan had been the latest of four boys Loren tried

having relationships with. The first two had not wanted an all the time Daddy and boy situation, and Loren had agreed to try. Both went wrong because it wasn't who Loren was. Hugo had been a delight; he was a boy through and through. Loren had thought they would be together forever because they seemed to mesh so well into each other's lives. They hardly needed to change anything. Unfortunately, Hugo hadn't understood the monogamy of the situation, and as soon as Loren found out, he had ended things with Hugo. That had devastated Loren.

By that point, he had lost his "mojo," as Ben said. He hadn't wanted to risk trying again with anyone, but one night, several months later, Ben had convinced Loren to accompany him to a Daddy and boy night at the club. Loren had gone, under protest, and had found Evan. Evan had been new to the city and finding his feet as a boy. Loren had happily taken him under his wing and explained everything he could about the lifestyle. Evan agreed to Loren's terms and added a couple of his own, and their relationship began.

Everything had been going swimmingly until eleven months later, Evan told Loren he was too over-bearing, too much, too there all the time. When Loren had asked what had changed from the beginning of their relationship to then, Evan had avoided the question.

Loren knew he could be overwhelming at times, but he couldn't change who he was. He had tried previously, and it hadn't worked either.

He exhaled, gripping his mug tighter. Loren knew himself. He needed a twenty-four-seven Daddy and boy relationship, or nothing. He'd have to live with being alone.

CHAPTER THREE

NATHAN

The coughing woke him. He pushed up onto his elbow and squinted across the moonlit room to where Robbie and Daisy were laid. "You okay, Daisy?"

He heard rustling. "She's not doing so good, Nathan. She's burning up." Robbie's voice trembled.

Nathan sat upright, rubbing the sleep from his eyes then from his whole face. He cleared his throat and tried to wake himself properly. "Have we got any antibiotics left?"

"No. We used them when I was down a few weeks back if you remember."

"Shit, yeah. I forgot about that." He exhaled. "Okay, let me get sorted, and I'll go see if I can find something."

"It's okay, I'll go." Nathan could see shadows moving and knew Robbie was getting up. "No, Robbie. I'll go. You stay and comfort her." He stood up, shivering in the chilled air. "You know the rules. If I'm not—"

"Back by six, you're not coming back. Yes, I get it." Robbie's voice was harsh. "You wouldn't have to give me those warnings if you didn't do what you did."

"Robbie…there's not much else I can do to get the kind of money we need to keep going out here."

Robbie sighed. "Sorry. I know. I'm worried about you. There are too many creeps out there."

"I'll be fine. I say it as a precaution, that's all." Nathan passed over his share of the remaining food and drink from the shopping two days ago. "See if you can get her to drink something. I'll grab some more on the way back."

"Thanks, man."

"No problem."

Zipping up his jacket and pulling the collar up as far as he could, Nathan braced for the cold, slipping out the door and closing it solidly behind him. The shack was drafty as all hell, but it sheltered them from the worst of it. Quickening his footsteps in the shadowy night, he hustled through the streets to his usual workplace. Stopping at a public toilet, he spent a few minutes preparing himself—some men were too impatient to be kind—then carried on his way. Inhaling deeply before turning into the alley, he altered his stroll and opened his jacket, pasting a serene smile on his face, masking his real feelings.

Antibiotics were not easily found on the streets, and he knew he would have to pay over-the-odds for them. Because of the price issue, his work would have to be the kind he refused for the most part—he had a little dignity after all was said and done.

Scanning the clients, he chose his target, sauntering over with an enhanced sway to his hips. "Hey, handsome. You seem like someone who could rock my world." He paused in front of the guy, licking his lips suggestively and stroking his arm.

The guy's pupils blew wide, and his breathing increased. "Hell, yes."

"What can I be for you tonight, gorgeous?" Nathan could see the lust for control take over the guy's expression: the slight narrowing of his gaze, the licking of his lips, the extension of his spine, making him taller.

The guy leaned forward. "You can be the bitch who stands there and takes it while I pound into you."

Nathan bit his lip, a little turned on despite the surroundings. He loved a man who took control. He loved it more when they looked after him as well as themselves. This would be the former rather than the latter but still. Mmm. He lowered his voice to a whisper. "I am that bitch."

"How much?" The guy closed the gap and rested his hands at Nathan's hips, grinding his hard cock against Nathan's stomach. He reminded Nathan of a bear. He was tall, wide—be it from muscles or fat, Nathan had no idea—a full beard and moustache and shoulder-length hair.

"Sixty and you use a condom," Nathan replied.

"Forty."

Nathan pretended to think about it. "Fifty."

"Done." The guy shoved a hand into his pocket

and fanned out some bills. Nathan raised his eyebrows at the amount he had but said nothing. "Half now, half after." The bear shoved twenty-five pounds into Nathan's hands and shoved the rest into his pocket.

Pursing his lips, Nathan took the money. He usually made sure they paid upfront, but he needed the money too much to argue. "Follow me."

Turning on his heel, Nathan sauntered further through the alley towards the other end, which exited onto the main nightclub-and-bar-lined street. It was a lot darker there, but they'd have the semblance of privacy. Halting at a semi-comfortable perch, Nathan wheeled to face the bear.

Hands immediately grabbed his hips and pulled him close, a hard cock thrusting against Nathan. Those hands fumbled for Nathan's jeans. "Come on, baby. Let's see what you have for me."

Cold fingers pulled open his jeans and down his boxers, exposing him to the freezing air. "Fuck."

"Yeah, tell me about it. You feel amazing."

Nathan hadn't meant about the fucking. He spoke about the cold, but he carried on as if it was what he meant all along. "I'm ready for you."

The guy exhaled roughly, twisting Nathan to face away from him and pushing on his back.

Impatient, impatient. Nathan rolled his eyes but stuck his ass out further, humming in pretend delight. Well, kind of pretend. He enjoyed being manhandled sometimes.

A palm caressed his bare ass cheeks, massaging

intermittently and pulling them apart. "Look at you," the bear whispered reverently.

Nathan preened under the compliment. He felt the guy move closer, rubbing his fabric-covered cock against his crack. Nathan pressed back, moaning.

"Yesss." Hands left his body, and Nathan heard the familiar sounds of a belt, zip and wrapper. "This will be cold." Bear's voice was soothing.

Nathan's brow puckered. Why...? Oh. He was pleasantly surprised when the guy rubbed lube against his hole with a finger, preparing him. "Oh!" Pleasure, more from the care the guy took than from the situation, filled his body, and he found himself responding. He licked his dry lips as the man carefully stretched him. The tenderness in his ministrations had Nathan's emotions opening, his mind wishing for a different scenario.

"Right, bitch. Take it." The guy's tone had taken a different edge, and before Nathan could ready himself, the condom-covered shaft pushed in forcefully, taking Nathan's breath.

He slammed his hands further forward to halt his body's movement, pressing back against the guy.

"That's it, bitch. You take what I give you." The guy exhaled roughly in time with his thrusts.

"Fuck, yes." Nathan breathed erratically. If only this were real. If only this was his Daddy giving him what he needed in both ways—preparing and fucking him.

"Oh, yeah. Yes. You're so tight. Made just for me."

"Yes, I am. Just for you." Getting lost in the fantasy

wasn't his usual routine. But Nathan couldn't help it as the feelings of loneliness abated for a short time. The guy knew what he was doing and changed his angle. "Oh, fuck!"

"There we go. Let me feel your ass strangling my cock, baby."

The words pierced Nathan's brain, and he felt himself careen closer to his orgasm. He was surprised —not about climaxing with a client, but that he was there so fast. "Yes. Yes, please!

"Ah, fuck. Yes!"

Nathan was manhandled backwards once more, and, with a groan of satisfaction, the guy emptied himself into the condom. Trying to move, Nathan growled, his impending orgasm slowly losing steam as he was restrained.

"Fuck. That was fantastic." A hand slapped his ass after the guy pulled out of him, Nathan flinching away in surprise and annoyance.

Standing, Nathan pulled his underwear and jeans back into place. He clenched his jaw against the words he wanted to say and smirked at the bear. "Glad you were satisfied." The undercurrent of which was 'why the hell wouldn't you let me be satisfied, too?'

"Here." The guy held out some notes, and Nathan took it, squinting down to see thirty-five pounds. He glanced up, confused. "Worth it." The guy winked, pivoted and strode away, Nathan's annoyance going with him.

Frustrated and horny as he now was, Nathan decided he may as well find another client to make some money for food and drink. If Daisy was extremely ill, they needed to make sure they had enough for her to get through it.

Nathan tucked the money deep into his pocket and returned to the alley, sizing up the remaining customers. It was getting late, so he didn't have as much choice but saw one who resembled someone nice. Sashaying over, Nathan studied him up and down. Under normal circumstances, the guy would be his usual type. Maybe he could help Nathan *finish*.

"You look like someone who could help me." Nathan cocked his hip and tilted his head.

The guy's peak cap shadowed his face as he examined Nathan, revealing it again when he glanced up, nodding. He held out his hand. "Gray."

Eyebrows raising at the formality, Nathan shook Gray's hand. "Nathan."

"Nice to meet you, Nathan."

Narrowing his eyes, he stepped forward. "What can I do for you tonight?"

"I need to take the edge off." Gray's tone was melancholic, and Nathan wondered what he was going through to sound sad.

"I can do that." Not even discussing the price, Nathan led him back to his previous tryst's position.

"How much?" Gray asked.

"Fifty."

Gray nodded.

Nathan wasn't sure if it was easier or harder knowing the guy's name, but he continued, feeling the need to help the guy. He reached to undo his jeans, but

Gray halted him. Eyes connected with Gray's, Nathan dropped his hands, allowing Gray to release his cock from its confines. The cool air was welcomed this time with Nathan feeling a lot warmer.

Warm, calloused hands gripped Nathan's hips and turned him around, brushing across his ass, making Nathan inhale briskly. He automatically leaned forward, presenting his ass in his usual position.

He heard a shaky inhale and felt overwhelmingly aroused by the sound. Nathan closed his eyes, the feeling of being wanted, cared for, overpowering his usual distance from the activity.

Familiar sounds once more reached his ears, and Nathan prepared for the intrusion. Gray pressed his cock against Nathan's hole, fingers gripping his hips as Gray pushed forward slowly. Nathan was already on the edge, especially after being left high and dry last time, but this felt…more. It felt like he was being cared for.

He bit his lip against the words wanting to escape but groaned as Gray bottomed out.

"You okay?" Gray asked, voice husky and deep.

"Uh-huh," was all Nathan could manage.

Gray withdrew then pushed in again, a slow rhythm starting, and Nathan kept his mouth tightly closed, not wanting to break the unspoken rule of quiet. Gray's hands travelled the length of Nathan's spine underneath his jacket and t-shirt, and Nathan shivered.

If he ignored their surroundings, eyes closed as they were, Nathan could pretend he was bent over a table in a nice house, being fucked by his Daddy. The dream hardened his cock further until he could feel precome dripping from the tip. He wasn't going to last long.

"Yeah," he breathed, hardly making a sound.

Gray picked up his speed, the slap of skin against skin loud in their silence, and Nathan couldn't withhold his groans any longer.

"Fuck, yes."

Hands moved to his shoulders, pulling him back against Gray as he thrust his hips forwards but still no words.

"Yes. I'm gonna come. Yes, please, Daddy!" Nathan vocalised.

Seconds later, he felt himself falling forward and hitting his head.

CHAPTER FOUR

LOREN

Trudging down the street after having been harassed during dinner at Ben's house, Loren jumped as a guy ran out in front of him, exiting from an alley. He watched as the guy crossed the road and kept running. Shrugging and shaking his head, Loren drifted away again, only to hesitate when he heard a pain-filled groan coming from the same alley the guy had come from. Loren paused, not knowing what he could be getting himself into, but he didn't want to leave someone in pain if he could help them.

He squinted into the semi-darkness and fumbled to retrieve his phone, using the torch to light his way. Panning it from side to side, he followed the sounds until he reached a guy lying on his side on the concrete, hand to his head and trousers and underwear around his knees.

Loren was no prude. He knew the sex trade was

alive and well in Cambridge but had never come this close to it. If that was what this was. It could have been a mutual hook-up.

"Hey. Are you alright?" he asked the guy on the ground.

No answer apart from more groans.

Loren stepped closer, making sure to scratch his shoes across the gravel to indicate his presence.

"Are you okay?" he repeated.

"Fuck, my head." The response was quiet, he could only just hear it.

"Sir? I'm going to help you, okay? Let's get your clothes on so you don't freeze." Loren rested his phone against his bag on the floor in a way that the light could shine on them. He tentatively reached forward, ensuring he didn't touch the guy in any way except the waistband of his underwear and jeans as he pulled them up awkwardly. He managed to get them higher but not all the way, accompanied by the groans of the guy as it was, over his ass and cock, but couldn't lift the jeans far. Loren rested back on his heels. The guy hadn't flinched at the touch of Loren's hands, which pointed him closer to the sex trade theory.

"Sir? What happened? Do you need to go to the hospital?"

"No!" The voice was adamant, regardless of how quiet the sound.

"Does your head hurt?"

"Yes. Fell."

Yeah, right. "Can I take a look?" Loren had first

aid experience, but it was from over ten years ago. He didn't think things had changed too drastically.

More groans followed his question, and Loren didn't think the guy would let him check him over. But the guy shakily peeled his hands away.

Loren leaned closer after reaching for his phone. "Sorry, this might be a bit bright, but I need to see." He aimed the light to the man's forehead, finding a cut on the edge of his hairline where a lump was forming already. Loren winced, knowing the guy would undoubtedly have a pounding headache, if not already, the next day. "Okay. You've cut your head. You need to go to the hospital to get it checked out."

"No!" Dark eyes blinked up at him. "I'll be fine. I just need…" The guy trailed off as he attempted to sit up, groaned and laid back down.

"Let me help you to sit." Loren replaced his phone on his bag and shifted his position, sliding his hands under the guy's armpits and taking most of his weight. After a couple of stumbles, they managed to get the guy leaned against the alley wall. Loren fished out a handkerchief from his pocket and offered it to the guy.

"Thanks," the guy whispered.

"Care to tell me what happened?" Loren wasn't sure why he was so interested.

"I couldn't keep my mouth shut." He pressed the fabric to his head, grimacing and closing his eyes again.

"What do you mean?"

"It doesn't matter." The guy didn't elaborate.

Loren didn't know what to do. The guy was coherent, but Loren knew concussion was a possibility and didn't want to leave the guy alone. "What's your name?"

The dark-haired man tensed and flicked a frown his way, inspecting Loren up and down, then relaxing his shoulders once more. "Nathan."

"Nice to meet you, Nathan. I'm Loren."

"Loren? Where's that name from?"

Loren chuckled. "No idea, in all honesty. My parents were never vocal as to why they chose this particular unusual name." He observed Nathan grimace again. "We need to get your head checked. I'm not happy leaving you alone when you've bashed your head pretty badly."

"I'll be fine. You don't need to worry about me. I'll head back to my friends; they'll keep an eye on me." Nathan attempted to stand, but only managed to lean forward before he groaned and grabbed his head.

"Yeah, you'll be fine," Loren deadpanned. He was not letting the guy stay by himself. He could call a taxi and get Nathan to his friends. "Where do your friends live?"

"Um…in the city centre."

Loren hesitated, waiting for more information, but none was forthcoming. "Whereabouts in the city centre?"

"Why would I give you my address? I don't know you." Nathan glowered up at him.

Loren tilted his head, acknowledging the answer. "True. But I would've thought the fact I didn't take advantage of how I found you would speak for itself."

They locked gazes, a world of information passing between them in the silence. Finally, Nathan spoke, "I share a small...space with two of my friends, not far from here."

Loren narrowed his eyes. Turning over what he knew about Nathan so far, he presumed Nathan skirted the fact he was homeless. "Would you be willing to come home with me and have use of my spare room?"

Whipping his gaze toward him fast enough to have Loren wincing with the potential whiplash, Nathan stared at him open-mouthed. Loren waited for him to finish impersonating a fish and find his words.

"Why would you do that?"

"Do what?"

"Offer your house to a stranger?"

The heavily puckered brow made him look cute, Loren noted. He shrugged. "If I can help someone, why not do it? You don't need to worry about probing questions or me expecting 'benefits' from it. Just a place to go where you can recuperate, and I can ease my mind knowing I've not left you to die from concussion complications."

The silence surrounding them was tense, and Loren needed to move, the cold in the air making his muscles ache, but he didn't want to startle Nathan. He waited him out.

A throat cleared. "If you don't mind—" Nathan's voice cut off.

"I don't." Loren exhaled slowly, his shoulders relaxing under his thick coat. He had something he could now do to help...get Nathan to his house. Loren picked up his phone, opened an app and booked a taxi. As it was before midnight, most people were still in the pubs and clubs, so they had spare cars available quickly. "Okay. Let's get you on your feet and see how steady you are." Loren pocketed his phone and crouched in front of Nathan once more.

Sliding his hands behind Nathan's back, Loren tucked his hands under his arms and took most of Nathan's weight. He refused to acknowledge the sweet scent tickling his nose apart from a brief closure of his eyes. Then he was back to work. Nathan used one hand on the wall to help lever his body upright, and his other had hold of his jeans, luckily.

Or unluckily.

Loren shook his head to wipe the thought away, concentrating on steadying Nathan as he finally found his feet. "How are you doing?" Audible exhales and inhales were the reply. "Do you feel sick?"

Another exhale. "A little."

"Okay, rest back on the wall for a moment and breathe deeply." Loren manoeuvred Nathan until he was propped against the brick. He noticed Nathan still had hold of his jeans. Clearing his throat, he asked, "Would you like me to refasten your jeans?"

He watched as twin splashes of red appeared on each cheek, spreading down Nathan's neck as he tightly rolled his lips together. He nodded once, sharply.

Not wanting to make a fuss and show his embarrassment, Loren grabbed the waistband of the jeans, pulling them up and fastening the button and zipper.

He tried to be mechanical about it all, but he loved that Nathan allowed him to take care of him.

And that right there was one reason he should not have asked Nathan to stay with him.

Loren stepped back but kept an eye on Nathan's form in case he decided to dive for the ground.

"What do you do?"

Nathan's sultry tone wrapped around Loren's brain, and he briefly closed his eyes. This was such a bad idea. "I'm an accountant." He was unable to see the expression on Nathan's face. Loren was about to ask—he was sure—an inappropriate question when he heard the taxi driver shout from the mouth of the alleyway. "We're coming!" he bellowed back.

Stepping forward, Loren wrapped his arm around Nathan's waist, gripping his right hip, and threw Nathan's left arm over his shoulder, holding onto his wrist for leverage. Together they slogged towards the street. When Nathan stumbled, he grabbed hold of Loren's hand on his waist and never removed it. Loren tried to ignore the cold palm, though it felt so right against his hand.

Loren paused at the taxi as the driver opened the door to the back seat for them. "Is he alright?" the driver asked.

"Yes. He's cut his head, but we're going to get it sorted now." Loren's answer was short and succinct; he told the guy to mind his own business.

Helping Nathan into the low seats was not easy, but they managed without too many problems. Shutting the door, Loren hustled around to the other side and got in. He reached across Nathan to grab the seatbelt and buckled him in, aware of the scrutiny his new roommate gave him. After Loren buckled his own, he repeated his address to the driver, not because the driver didn't know where they were going, but because it gave his address to Nathan without fanfare in case he wanted to let anyone know where he was.

Speaking of, "Do you need to let anyone know where you are?" Loren eyed Nathan, watching him swallow and move his gaze to the passing scenery.

"No," he answered softly.

"What about your friends?"

"There's no way to contact them without going to see them."

"Nathan." He waited until Nathan peered at him. "Do you want to go and tell your friends where you are going to be?"

The only noise in the taxi was the sound of the radio playing softly from the front and the noise of the car on the road. Loren roamed his gaze across Nathan's face as he waited for his answer.

"No."

Loren nodded once and turned to his window, fighting to keep his hands where they were instead of reaching for Nathan.

They arrived at Loren's house quickly; he didn't live far from where he'd found Nathan. Loren paid for the taxi and helped Nathan down the path to his front door, opening it one-handed and holding tight to him as they crossed the threshold. He kicked the door closed behind them and guided Nathan to the stairs, switching lights on as they went.

"Let's take this slow. I don't want your head to hurt more. We'll get you situated in the spare room, and then we'll sort out your head."

Nathan made an acknowledging noise in the back of his throat as he stared at the floor, and Loren concentrated on their destination instead of the red tinges he saw twining through Nathan's strands of lighter-than-expected hair as it fell across his face.

Loren opened the bedroom door, flicking the light and helped Nathan across to the armchair. "Right. Sit here for a few minutes while I get some things sorted." He watched as Nathan rested back, his head naturally falling to one side with his eyes closed. "No falling asleep on me, Nathan," he said sternly.

Nathan's eyes flew open, his gaze finding Loren's immediately. An expression crossed his face, which Loren couldn't decipher, but he sat more upright in the chair. Loren nodded and exited the bedroom for the main bathroom, where he kept a first aid kit and pain relief. Grabbing both, he stalked back to the spare room, finding Nathan in the same position as he left him. *Good boy*.

Loren cleared his throat at the thought and busied himself with sorting through the kit, finding the items he needed to clean the cut. He turned to the young man and, after a brief hesitation, kneeled at his feet, watching as Nathan's eyes flared wide and a flush crept back into his cheeks.

"I need to clean the cut," Loren whispered, not

wanting to break the haze of…whatever this was.

Nathan nodded but didn't move.

Taking the nod as agreement, Loren lifted his hand to grip Nathan's chin between his thumb and finger. The first proper feel of Nathan's skin under Loren's fingertips had his breath catching; it was soft and cool, although beginning to warm now that they were inside. He dabbed at the cut, apologising when Nathan hissed and pulled away, but cleaned it out properly. It wasn't as deep as he first thought, but the developing bruise was not going to look pretty on such an unblemished face.

"There you go. It's not as deep as I first thought, but it's going to hurt like hell in the morning, I reckon." Loren stood and reached for the paracetamol, passing over a cup of water he'd also retrieved.

Watching as Nathan took the pain relief, Loren's heart swelled with the unexpected submission.

"Thank you." Nathan's voice was quiet, and Loren hoped he was not having second thoughts.

"You're welcome. I haven't put a bandage on it yet because I wondered if you'd want to wash up a bit before we get your settled into bed?" Loren busied himself with clearing up the contents of the first aid kit, not wanting to hover, even though it went against his instincts.

"Yes, please. I don't…" Nathan stopped, which had Loren glancing at him, eyebrows raised.

When he didn't continue, Loren asked, "You don't, what?" Loren watched as Nathan fiddled with his jacket, studying the floor. "Nathan." Brown eyes flicked up to his immediately, and Loren felt a sense of satisfaction flow through him. He waited.

Nathan swallowed. "I don't have any other clothes," he muttered.

Possessiveness went through Loren. "You get yourself cleaned up, and I'll grab you something to wear. Take a shower if you want one. There is a seat in there you can take into the shower with you." Loren headed to the door, indicating Nathan should follow, although keeping an eye on him to ensure he was steady.

Nathan nodded, feet shuffling towards him. Loren showed him the bathroom and left him to it. He strode to his bedroom and picked out some joggers, boxers and a t-shirt. He took some time and sat on his bed to get his thoughts in order.

Loren rubbed both hands over his face, resting his elbows on his thighs, before dropping his hands. He would admit he was attracted to Nathan. He ticked all the boxes of what Loren wanted from a boy, but there was no way Loren would ever approach him about it. He'd told Nathan he wouldn't expect benefits from this arrangement, and he would stick to it, regardless of how much he wanted to take Nathan down to the mattress and show him exactly what Daddy could do for him.

Pressing against his semi-hard shaft, trying to calm it, Loren took a few breaths. Once he was less aroused, he picked up the clothes and wandered down the hallway. He heard the shower running and left the clothes on a stool outside the door and headed to the kitchen to make something to eat.

CHAPTER FIVE

NATHAN

Using the bath chair, Nathan showered carefully, trying to keep the shampoo from entering his cut. His mind wandered to Loren. Initially, he wondered what the guy received from this arrangement, but the way Loren was so careful around him and focused on caring for him made Nathan's stomach flutter, and he was no longer concerned. Hidden under the stream of water as he was, Nathan admitted it was nice being taken care of. It was why he'd agreed. His boy personality loved it, which was exactly the kind of relationship he wanted to be in.

He needed to remember not to get comfortable, though. Loren was being kind, and Nathan would be back out on the streets tomorrow.

Ignoring his semi-hard cock, Nathan dried himself off, wrapping the towel around his waist and inspecting his head. There would be a huge bruise there by tomorrow, without a doubt.

Nathan peered around. There were no clothes in the bathroom, so he knew Loren hadn't come in when he'd been in the shower. He could've put them in Nathan's room. Clutching at the knot, Nathan opened the door, pausing when he saw the pile on the stool to the side of the door.

Nathan beamed and picked them up, scanning the hallway towards the stairs where he could hear Loren pottering around. Retreating again, he closed the door, placing the garments on the counter. They were too big for him, but Loren had chosen jogging bottoms that could be cinched tighter around the waist, and it would help with keeping them on. As Nathan got to the boxers, he hesitated. Under normal circumstances, he would ignore them and not use them because they belonged to someone else, but because they were Loren's...Nathan bit his lip, his breathing increasing.

The idea of wearing something intimate that belonged to his—temporary—*Daddy* was more than he could take. He slid them on, closing his eyes and rolling his lips inwards to withhold the moan. His cock would be too difficult to ignore if he didn't calm himself down.

Quickly dressing in the other items, Nathan towel-dried his hair once more and rested the towel on the radiator. Barefoot, he wandered slowly towards the stairs, hesitating when he saw Loren ascending.

"You should be getting back into bed, Nathan,"

Loren chastised, indicating the spare room with his head, carrying a tray in his hands.

Nathan flushed, barely restraining the urge to say, "Yes, Daddy." But, remembering how that went earlier in the evening, he turned on his heels and held the door open for Loren, receiving a pleased look and a "Thank you." The butterfly feeling in his stomach intensified with the praise.

"I brought you a slice of toast and a glass of milk to help you sleep. Jump into bed." The words were not an order, but Nathan felt the need to obey regardless.

"You didn't have to make me anything." Nathan sat against the bed's headboard, legs stretched out in front, hands twiddling in his lap.

"I know, but you need to keep your strength up." Loren sat on the edge of the bed, his thigh resting against Nathan's knee, and placed the tray on Nathan's legs.

Surveying what was in front of him, Nathan watched as they became blurry, and he tried to stop the tears from overflowing.

"Hey, now. What's all this about?" Loren rested his hand on Nathan's forearm, stroking his skin with his thumb.

Nathan used his other hand to wipe under his eyes, brushing away the evidence of his foolishness. "I'm fine." He attempted a smile.

Loren stared at him, gaze strong and resolute. "Tell me what's wrong." His words brooked no argument, although not a firm order.

Nathan sniffed and swallowed, licking his bottom

lip, debating what to say. There was no way he would admit to wanting this more with every breath he took. He went with the partial truth and hoped Loren would leave it at that. "I've not had someone look after me for so long, it's difficult to accept."

The hand on his arm squeezed, and a soft inhale preceded Loren's words, "Are you homeless, Nathan?"

Nathan said nothing, eyes fixed on the food this amazing man had made for him.

"Nathan."

Closing his eyes, dislodging a stray tear, Nathan nodded as it rolled down his cheek.

"Okay. Eat up, and we'll get you into bed. A good night's sleep will do you a world of good."

True to his word, Loren watched as Nathan ate and drank every bite. He then attached a dressing to Nathan's forehead and—literally—tucked Nathan into bed. Nathan watched as Loren picked up the empty tray and headed to the door.

"Thank you—" Nathan caught himself before he added a word that would change everything. He couldn't deal with a beating, not after Loren had been so kind up until now.

Loren pivoted around, the grin on his face matching the shine in his eyes. "You're welcome, Nathan. Get some sleep. I'm right down the hall if you need anything." With that, he switched off the light and closed the door, leaving Nathan to sleep.

⟵————————⟶

Nathan hadn't thought he'd be able to sleep with the surroundings being different from his usual, but when he woke the next day, he couldn't remember anything after Loren closed the door. Sitting up, he stretched and yawned, then winced as his forehead pinched. He had no idea what time it was, he only knew it was daytime because the sun peeked past the edges of the closed curtains.

Wanting to find Loren, despite the uncertainty flowing through him, Nathan headed down the stairs after briefly visiting the bathroom. He could smell bacon and toast and followed his nose to the kitchen. Hesitating at the entrance, he watched Loren in motion. The radio played songs Nathan had heard when he'd been in various shops—he assumed it was recent pop music or such— but his eyes were captivated by the man moving his head and hips in time with the music, whilst moving something around in a pan on the stove.

Distracted as Loren was, Nathan took the time to study him. Thick, black hair covered his head, but Nathan noticed a few lighter streaks catching in the light, and a body that was filled out in all the right places as far as Nathan was concerned. Tilting his head, Nathan examined Loren objectively. Nathan considered him to be an average type of guy, especially if he included the dark-rimmed glasses, smart trousers and v-neck jumpers.

All in all, Loren was very appealing.

Nathan must have made some noise because the

next thing he knew, he was pinned by the bright blue gaze of the owner of his appreciation.

"Hey. I was going to come and check on you again once I'd made some food. How are you doing?" Loren beamed directly at Nathan, making his knees weak.

"I'm good." All of what Loren said finally registered. "Um…check on me again?"

Loren nodded and turned back to the stove, removing the bacon from the pan and placing it on a plate. "Yeah, I've been checking on you every two hours all night. Do you know you sleep like the dead!" He laughed, lifting a plate and passing it over to Nathan. "Brunch is served."

Nathan's gaze widened as he scanned the room for a clock, seeing it was eleven in the morning. "Woah. I haven't slept that long in a long time."

"Well, your head injury coupled with a warm bed and painkillers helped." He reached the plate out to Nathan, indicating for him to sit at the breakfast bar. "Here. Eat up."

Nathan sat, floored by the amount of food he had in front of him. "I don't…"

Loren glanced at him when he didn't continue. "Don't what?"

"I don't know if I'm going to be able to eat all this."

Loren smiled. "Eat what you can. But you need to keep your energy up." Loren brought over his plate, which had half the amount of food on it.

Half-wondering why he needed high energy levels, Nathan ate the pancakes, bacon, beans and toast. He had not eaten food like that in a long time. The thought reminded him of Robbie and Daisy. They were probably really worried about him. He hoped Daisy wasn't too sick. He felt bad for not taking any medication back to them, but he knew it couldn't be helped.

"What's wrong?" Loren reached across the space and rested his hand over the top of Nathan's.

Nathan glanced at him and back to the plate. "My friends are likely to be worried about me." He remembered something Loren had said earlier in their conversation and frowned over at Loren. "Why did you check on me every two hours last night?"

Loren's eyebrows rose. "You have a head injury; I needed to be sure you were still breathing whilst in my care."

Mouth falling open, Nathan apologised, "I'm sorry. I never thought about you having to do that. You must be knackered." He put his cutlery down and stood. "I'll get out of your way, and you can get some more rest."

"Sit."

He was sat back in his seat before he'd consciously registered the order. He bit his lip as he stared at Loren.

"Now, firstly, you don't need to be sorry. I was happy to do it. It was more for my peace of mind than anything else. I'm sorry if you feel I intruded on your space, but I had to be sure you were okay."

"No—"

"I should have told you I would be doing it. Although I don't think it mattered because you were delirious every time I woke you." Loren smirked. "It was cute."

"I don't remember waking up at all."

"You were well gone. An alarm right by your ear wouldn't have woken you." Loren snickered.

Nathan flushed. "Sorry. I was comfortable."

Loren's smile softened. "I'm glad." He picked up his fork and prepared to eat again. "Secondly, you don't need to get out of my way. You are welcome to stay for as long as you need to."

Leaving Nathan with those words, Loren shovelled some food into his mouth, gaze fixed on his plate, leaving Nathan stunned.

"Wha–?" Nathan inhaled, gaze roaming the space in front of him. He couldn't understand why this stranger offered him the room to stay in. He would have loved to accept it, but Nathan hated being a burden. "Thank you for the offer, but I'm fine."

Loren nodded slowly but didn't reply, just carried on eating.

Nathan wasn't sure what to say, so he picked up his cutlery and finished off his food. And he was immensely glad he had when Loren gifted him with a grin which lit up the house.

"I've washed and dried your clothes. I thought it would be better to get the dirt off the knees of your jeans rather than let it dry on." Loren picked up the plates and moved back to the kitchen area, placing them in the sink. "Can I have another check of your head?"

"Sure."

Loren stepped to his side, and Nathan twisted on the seat until they were facing each other. Carefully, Loren reached up and peeled off the plaster. "It looks okay, actually. The bruise is nasty, but it doesn't take away from your charm."

Nathan tried to prevent his heart from galloping out of his chest and into the hands of the man in front of him. His whole body flushed under the scrutiny of this stranger, but he couldn't stop the feelings brewing up. He wished Loren could be his Daddy, and he had no idea if Loren knew what a Daddy was, let alone was interested in him that way. He needed to get out of there.

Loren stepped back, and Nathan missed his nearness. "Sorry, I shouldn't have said that. I was trying to make you laugh."

Frowning, Nathan eyed Loren, recalling what he'd said, he flushed again. "It's fine."

"Right. I have to go to work." Nathan's heart fell at his words. He watched as Loren went to the front door, reached for something out of the tray on the entrance table and strolled back to him. Loren held out his hand. "Here is a spare key. Make yourself comfortable and get some more rest. I'm not sure exactly what time I'll be back, but I'll bring some food with me."

Shaking his head, Nathan stood. "I don't need a key. I'll get ready to leave now."

"No. You need more rest before you head out into this weather."

"I've been in worse."

"That may be the case, but I would like you to stay

out of the rain while your head is healing." Loren's gaze hooked him in.

Nathan worried his bottom lip, torn between being warm and sheltered, and not being a burden.

"It's not up for debate." Loren pushed the key into his palm. "In case you need it. At any time. Now or the future."

"But—"

Loren silenced him with a finger to his lips. "No, Nathan. Rest, relax, eat, sleep. I will be back later."

Nathan lowered his gaze to the floor, nodding slowly, feeling every slide of Loren's finger against his lips and trying not to react. Or at least, trying not to let his body show how he wanted to react.

Loren shuffled away. Nathan was frozen to the spot until he heard the front door close behind Loren. He sank into the seat he had previously occupied and stared around the house. Overwhelmed by the magnitude of the gift Loren had given him, he couldn't do anything but think over their entire interaction since the previous night.

Now that he was alone and somewhat rested, he could see Loren being the perfect Daddy for him. But there was no way Nathan would bring it up into the conversation. No way at all. That's the first way to get yourself kicked out—as the prior incident highlighted.

But it didn't stop Nathan from wanting Loren with a fierce ache. Nathan stood on shaky knees, deciding he would enjoy a peaceful day.

Several hours later, after a small lunch, which was a feast to him, he elected to shower. Two showers in less than twenty-four hours was a record for him, but he would enjoy every minute of it before he had to go back out there.

Flicking the shower to hot, Nathan stripped out of the clothes, resting them on the counter to wear again afterwards. It might seem stupid to put clothes on he'd worn before the shower, but he was used to being in clothes with several days' dirt on them. He didn't want to rifle through Loren's stuff for more, and Loren hadn't told him where he'd put his newly cleaned clothes.

Nathan stood under the spray, groaning with the luxury of hot water provided at pressure. It soothed his muscles more than anything else. Well, almost anything else. With that in mind, his cock hardened. Rubbing soap over his body in leisurely strokes heightened his arousal. He slid a finger across a nipple, dropping his head back with the stiffening of his already hard shaft. His hands smoothed over his slick body, his palms caressing his nubs each time he passed, getting closer and closer to his target.

"Fuck," he breathed. When he finally circled the base of his cock, he squeezed, staving off the threatening orgasm. Nathan rested one palm against the tiled wall, shifted to let the water beat onto his back and stroked his other hand up to the head of his cock. Using the tips of his finger, he teased his head repeatedly before sliding his fingers around to grasp himself then he slid them down his cock. His knees trembled with the pleasure streaming through his body, and he knew he wouldn't be able to hold back much longer.

Sliding his whole palm around his cock, he stroked in earnest, his mind taking him to the one thing he knew he couldn't have but wanted all the same. Loren —his Daddy—behind him, allowing Nathan the ecstasy of Loren's hands on his cock, giving him pleasure.

Permitting him to come.

"Fuck! Yes! Ah, god, yes!"

Nathan painted the tile with his release, barely keeping himself upright with the strength of it. Panting heavily, he rested his head against the wall.

CHAPTER SIX

LOREN

L oren entered the house, hoping to find Nathan in residence, although his head told him Nathan had gone. He stood in the hallway, listening, his whole body relaxing at the sound of the shower. Exhaling softly, he closed his eyes briefly, nodded and, balancing the bags in his arms, strode to the kitchen.

He'd picked up Chinese on the way home, and not knowing what Nathan enjoyed, he'd bought a variety. Setting it up on the table with plates and cutlery, he ascended the stairs to tell Nathan the food was ready, but his feet froze on the top step when the sounds of heavy breathing, curse words and pleasurable sounds filtered through the closed door.

Inhaling roughly, it took everything in him to turn around and go back to the kitchen. He'd managed to stay at the café a lot longer than he thought he would, but he was home earlier than he usually as it was only three-thirty. Loren needed to ignore what he'd heard and carry on as normal.

Easier said than done when the man in question entered the room with a deer in headlights expression. Schooling his features, Loren smiled. "I brought Chinese. Hope you like it."

Nathan swallowed, then nodded.

"I think tonight we should put on a movie and eat Chinese. What do you think?" Loren was trying to keep Nathan here; he knew he was. He also knew Nathan would have to leave at some point, but Loren wasn't ready for it to be now. He'd figure out some way of keeping Nathan here for another day, at least.

"Sounds good," came the quiet reply.

"Come, choose what you want, and I'll get the trays. We can eat in the living room." Loren indicated the food, turning his back to open the cupboard for the lap trays he often used when he was on his own. When he faced Nathan again, it was to find him hovering over the dishes, not having chosen anything. "Do you not like them?" Loren was worried because Nathan had been on the street that his taste buds had changed.

"I..." Nathan swallowed audibly. "I wasn't sure what I could have."

Inwardly, Loren preened at the idea Nathan needed reassurance from him. Outwardly, he smiled. "Whatever you want—" He cut off his final words, *sweet boy*.

Biting his lip, Nathan took a small sample of each dish, which was not close to enough for him, but Loren would rectify it later. He watched Nathan's movements to determine which ones he enjoyed best and would fix him another plate. Loren had a strong need to take care of him while he was here.

The thought soured his mood some. He created his plate and directed Nathan to the living room. "What would you like to watch?"

"Anything. I'm not up on new films. You pick."

Loren didn't like the reminder Nathan hadn't had the luxuries he was entitled to. He picked a comedy with some action in it as well.

They settled on the two-seater sofa, close but not close enough according to Loren's mind. Loren kept his awareness on Nathan throughout the first part of the film, though. After around half an hour, Loren stood, gathering the plates. "I'm going to get a drink. Keep watching, I'll be back in a few."

He stalked to the kitchen. First, he made a cup of tea for himself, which he added to the tray with a couple of bottles of water and a glass of milk, then he made Nathan another plate of food. He stood at the island counter, breathing deeply several times, trying to brush away the feeling of rightness permeating the air. It wasn't an easy situation to be in, and he had no idea how to navigate his way through the maze. He'd love to see where this could go, but how could he bring up the fact he was a Daddy. Nobody outside of the clubs had ever heard about it, except obviously Ben.

Taking a final breath, Loren carted the tray back to the living room, finding Nathan sitting with his legs tucked underneath him.

"Are you cold?" Loren asked, frowning.

"A little."

Loren placed the tray on the coffee table and grabbed the throw from the armchair. He laid it over Nathan's legs, and, asking him to lift his arms, tucked it around his torso. Turning back to the table, he reached for the plate of food and passed it over, resting the cup of milk on the small side table next to where Nathan sat.

"What—?" Nathan's puckered brow expressed his confusion.

"I thought you might be hungry. There's plenty left." Loren sat himself back on his side of the sofa, ignoring the scrutiny Nathan gave him and drank his tea. Out of the corner of his eye, he saw Nathan hesitate then dig into the food. Loren hid his grin in his cup.

By the time the film had finished, Nathan was fast asleep, neck tilted at the most uncomfortable angle. Loren knew what he wanted to do—carry him to bed —but he needed to try and wake him instead.

"Nathan?" Loren shook the boy's shoulder. All he received was a slight change of position. He hadn't been joking when he'd told Nathan he slept like the dead; apparently, this wouldn't be any different. Loren would get his wish after all.

Standing, he gently pulled the throw off, discarding it into his empty seat, and, for a moment, studied the enigma that was Nathan. Smiling gently, he reached down, sliding one hand beneath his knees and the other around his back.

As Loren pulled Nathan against him, Nathan

rested his head on his shoulder, making a snuffling noise into his neck. Loren's heart grew more. Gently shifting Nathan closer, Loren drifted towards the stairs. As light as Nathan was, Loren would have no problem climbing them. He took his time, wanting to keep Nathan in his arms as long as possible. Loren laid Nathan on the soft mattress, lifting the duvet from beneath to cover him. He crouched next to the bed, watching as Nathan shifted, clutching the pillow closer and snuggling down.

Loren stayed there, listening to Nathan's breathing and reached a hand forward to brush gently at his hair. Pulling back once more, Loren rubbed a hand across his mouth, hiding his frown. He wanted nothing more than to be able to keep Nathan. Not in the kidnapping sense, but to care for him…feed him…love him.

He watched Nathan for a few more breaths, rising with reluctance. Standing in the open doorway, he glanced back, his heart overwhelmed with the emotion rising towards this…boy…after such a short time. Sighing, he closed the door and wandered back to the living room, cleaning up their dishes and taking them to the kitchen. His mouth turned up at the corners when he realised Nathan had cleared his plate the second time and drank all the milk.

Setting the kitchen to rights, the dishwasher rumbling in the background, he grabbed his work bag and settled himself at the table. There was no way he'd be able to sleep right at that moment, and the usual monotony of his job should be able to take his mind off the dilemma he found himself in.

<———————————>

Loren entered the house to an eerie silence, his heart hammering once more at the thought Nathan might have left. His bag fell softly to the floor as his shoulders dropped. That morning had started with an apology from Nathan for staying another night when he'd planned on heading out. Loren had reassured him he was welcome to stay as long as he needed to, as Loren had told him previously. Nathan had seemed unsure, and Loren had sweetened the deal by enticing Nathan with a home-cooked meal that night. By the time Loren had left for work—at the library, this time—he'd persuaded Nathan to stay until after they'd eaten at least.

Or so he'd thought.

He climbed the stairs with leaden feet, not wanting to see the proof of the emptiness of the house but needing to all the same. He headed towards the spare room, halting when a sound caught his attention. Spinning his head towards the bathroom, Loren paused, listening for more sounds. When another small noise sounded, Loren changed direction. He stood outside the bathroom door, hearing heavy breathing and movement inside.

Heart beating rapidly, his breathing increased as he connected what he heard with the images they could represent. He'd ignored hearing Nathan masturbate the previous day, but he was too close to leave now. Not in control of his movements at that point, Loren leaned forward. The sounds intensified, words becoming more distinguishable, shocking him with their content.

"Fuck, Daddy. Yes, that's it. Harder, please, Daddy, harder!" Nathan's voice was heavy with arousal, and Loren could imagine the expression of ecstasy on his face.

He leaned his forehead against the door, trying to curb his arousal, though, his cock was more than evident in his trousers. He pressed a palm against it, trying to ease the pressure, with the sounds of pleasure heightening on the other side of the door.

As he did, the door shifted and swung open, Loren just stopping himself falling inside.

His gaze landed on a vision that would forever be etched into his memory.

Nathan kneeled in the empty bath, naked, and fucking himself on a dildo. *Loren's* dildo. The one which can be stuck to certain surfaces to give the user a better experience.

"Fuck," he breathed, gaze locked with Nathan's movements.

Nathan's gaze flicked to his, his eyes widening then narrowing. Loren wondered why, until he heard it, "Yes, Daddy. Fuck, yes!" Nathan's cry of release reverberated around the tiled room, and Loren wanted to hear the sound forever. He watched as Nathan's release painted the bath and Nathan's hand, which had been wrapped around his thick cock.

Once the sound died down, the only thing Loren

could hear was their united breathing. Gaze locked with Nathan's, Loren took a chance.

"Did I say you could come?" Silence greeted his words.

Loren backed out of the door until Nathan whispered, "Sorry, Daddy."

Breathing a sigh of relief, Loren let his Daddy personality take control. "Get dried and wait in your bedroom." Loren left to retrieve the clothes he'd bought Nathan the previous day. And to calm down a little until he faced Nathan again. He noticed the top drawer of his chest was cracked open and understanding came. Loren nodded, the decision made, and headed to Nathan, this time with a different dynamic in mind for them.

Entering, he saw Nathan waiting in the room, towel around his waist, shuffling from foot to foot, vibrating with energy despite his recent release.

"Good boy." He placed the bag on the bed, standing close to Nathan, but not near enough to touch. They needed to clear the air first. "Why were you in my room?" he demanded.

Turning wide eyes towards Loren, Nathan wrung his hands together. Loren stepped in front of him, reaching to hold his hands still. Nathan stared at him, licking his lips. "I...I spilt coffee on the top I was wearing, and I wasn't sure where you had put my clothes. I didn't think you'd mind if I got another one. When I saw..." Nathan trailed off, a beautiful blush suffusing his cheeks and neck. "I'm sorry. It was wrong. I'll get dressed and leave." Nathan tried to turn, but Loren gripped his hands tighter. Their gazes locked once more, a wealth of information being taken and received.

Loren squeezed Nathan's hands, then let go. "Let's get you dressed, shall we?" Loren reached for the bag, riffling through the contents and choosing a pair of grey joggers and a blue short-sleeved t-shirt with a cartoon character on them. "Would you like to choose your underwear?" He laid out several pairs of briefs in different colours, so Nathan could choose.

Nathan frowned at the clothes before smiling softly and biting his lip, a trait Loren would cure him of. Nobody bruised that lip but him—he hoped. He watched as Nathan reached his hands across the selection and picked up the orange pair, surprising Loren. He'd expected him to be a bit more subdued.

"Perfect." Loren took the briefs from Nathan and crouched near his feet, so close to Nathan's cock, he had to use all his restraint not to touch. "Rest your hands on my shoulders and lift your foot." Nathan obeyed, and Loren pulled the briefs to Nathan's shin. "Other leg." Nathan replaced his left foot and lifted his right, repeating the process. As his foot found the floor once more, Loren slid the underwear up Nathan's legs, discarding the towel and pulling the waistband over his ass and cock. "Are you comfortable?"

"Yes, Daddy," was the soft reply.

Loren turned back to the chosen clothes, briefly closing his eyes with the pleasure strumming through him at those words. "Let's do it again with your trousers, sweet boy." They repeated their actions, this time, Loren slid his hands up along the outside of Nathan's thighs, watching the goosebumps follow in his wake and feeling Nathan tremble. Loren swallowed and stood quickly, his arousal humming along his veins. "Arms up." He pulled the t-shirt over Nathan's head and arms. "There we go, sweet boy. Let's get you some food." Ignoring his arousal, Loren took Nathan's hand and pulled him out of the room and towards the breakfast bar in the kitchen. "Sit."

Loren didn't think about what he did, other than to acknowledge he needed to show Nathan what he wanted, and this was the only way he knew of doing it. He needed Nathan to understand what Loren offered.

Bustling around the kitchen, trying to settle his nerves, Loren cut up some vegetables, throwing them in the tray with the chicken and placing it in the oven. After, he retrieved some fruit. He paused, momentarily, then pivoted towards a drawer. Pulling out a brand-new colouring book and crayons, he hesitated before sliding them across to Nathan. Not making eye contact, he turned back to making the dinner.

Loren knew what he wanted, but he needed to see what Nathan wanted, too. They had not talked yet; he didn't know what Nathan wanted out of this. But Loren needed to get it all out in the open, which he would do as soon as they'd eaten. He pulled down a cup, filled it with milk and twisted around to place it next to Nathan.

He froze in place when he saw Nathan sat there, arms wrapped around the colouring book with tears running down his face.

Hurrying to round the counter, Loren put the cup down. "Sweetheart, what's wrong?" He sat on the seat next to Nathan, smoothing a hand along his back. He had no idea what he'd done wrong. Maybe Nathan wasn't a boy who liked colouring. "I'm sorry if I—"

"No!" Nathan's voice was wet with tears, and he audibly swallowed. "No. You don't need to be sorry. I…I…" He cleared his throat. "I've never had anyone care for me the way you have while I've been here. I…I know some of what I want but finding someone who understands has never happened."

"What do you want, Nathan?" Apparently, they were talking about this now rather than later.

"I want someone to help me look after myself. I want to be able to…" he indicated the colouring book with his chin, "do some colouring or read comics to relax and forget about things." He rushed on, "I don't want the nappies and toys…at least I don't think so." Nathan frowned. "I'm not sure about that."

"You don't have to know everything right now, Nate." The nickname rolled off Loren's tongue but sounded right. Seeing the grin on Nathan's face as he lifted his chin, it appeared he liked the sound of it, too. "We can work it out as we go along. If you want to." Loren hoped Nathan did.

"I would."

Loren's heart soared at the words. "The things I need you to be sure about are that you want to try this and that you are honest about things. If, at any time, you are unsure or overwhelmed, you need to tell me."

"Yes, Daddy," Nathan replied shyly.

"Good boy." Loren wanted to seal the deal with a kiss but thought it better if he waited for Nathan to indicate he was ready. He stood. "Let me finish cooking, okay."

"Okay, Daddy." Nathan wiped at his face and placed the book in front of him. Loren moved the chopping board and fruit over to the breakfast bar; he could watch Nathan while he cut up the fruit. Nathan opened the colouring book to the first page and flattened the cover until it stayed flat. He pulled out the crayons, choosing blue, and rested his right hand against the book. Loren paused. He hadn't realised Nathan was left-handed. Not that it mattered, but it was a new piece of Nathan for Loren to file away for later.

He watched as Nathan meticulously coloured the balloon, the tip of his tongue visible through his teeth, wholly focused as he was. Loren tilted his head; he hadn't been this content for a long while. Refocusing on the fruit, he finished the fruit bowls and turned to the oven. Pulling out the tray, he checked the contents, replacing them as they needed a little longer. Loren took a breath and pivoted around to face Nathan, finding him watching Loren.

"Are you okay, sweet boy?" Loren tilted his head.

"Yes, Daddy. I made a picture for you."

"Thank you, Nate." He took the proffered book, seeing the neat colouring of several balloons being held in a young boy's hand. "It's great. Thank you so much." Loren slid the book back to Nathan. "Let's get this cleared away."

Nathan nodded and with a serene expression, replaced the crayons he had used in their box and pushed them across the table to Loren, who put them in the drawer where they lived.

"Good boy. Now, let's wash our hands. Dinner will be ready in a couple of minutes."

CHAPTER SEVEN

NATHAN

Nathan's heart felt full to bursting with everything that had happened over the last couple of hours. Naturally, Loren catching him using the dildo in the bathroom was *not* what he had planned, but it ended up with a result he couldn't argue with. Loren was a Daddy. Nathan could not believe his luck. He felt a little silly about his mini-breakdown, but Loren was so understanding—as a Daddy should be. And being able to colour, under Loren's watchful eye, was such an amazing experience.

Dinner was blissful. Not only because he was able to have a meal without having to *work* for it first, but because they talked. Not about anything in particular, but about the things they both enjoyed. Nathan had opened up about Robbie and Daisy—the only nod to the homelessness situation he was in—talking about them as a couple. He felt bad about not having been to see them to explain.

"We could go there tonight if you want to?" Loren's voice broke into his musings. "You could collect some of your things."

They had yet to discuss what the plan was for them. Nathan had assumed he'd head back out tonight and, over the next few weeks, get to know Loren more before progressing any further. Loren had a different idea.

Nathan bit his lip. "What things do I need to collect?"

Loren put his knife and fork down, crossing his arms loosely and resting his elbows on the table edge. "I don't like the idea of you being out there. I've been thinking about whether you might want to move in here. Into the spare room." Loren held up a hand when Nathan began to talk. "You don't have to start any kind of relationship with me. I'm not forcing you to do it in payment for the room. The room is yours, free and clear, regardless of our…situation."

Nathan studied his plate, moving the food around with his fork as he thought about what Loren had said. His life would be more comfortable if he stayed here, but he felt…unworthy. He'd done some demeaning things since he'd been on the streets. Yes, they ensured his survival, but it didn't mean they were any less embarrassing. He couldn't believe Loren would want anything to do with him, but it sounded as if Loren wanted him there.

Thoughts were tumbling around and around in his brain.

"Nathan." The quiet but authoritative voice captured Nathan's attention once more, encouraging him to face Loren. "You don't have to make a big decision right now. You are welcome to think about it, but I would love it if I could make your life a little easier while you do think."

Nathan's gaze roamed Loren's face, seeing the wrinkled brow, ocean blue eyes under sexy thick black glasses and the full lips which spoke with so much care. He nodded with a bite of his lip. "I'll stay while I decide."

Watching as he was, Nathan saw pure joy spread across Loren's features, making him appear immediately younger than…whatever age he was.

"Shall we visit with Robbie and Daisy?" Loren pressed, reclaiming his cutlery and continuing to eat.

"Yes, please, Daddy." Nathan had lots to tell them.

⟵——————————⟶

"Here."

Nathan saw the coat Loren held out towards him. "What's this?"

"Something a little warmer than your jacket." Loren held the coat open for Nathan to slide his arms into, and immediately warmth encased him, more so when Loren turned him to face him and proceeded to zip up said coat.

"Thank you." Nathan couldn't remember a time he had been warm—well, when he was on his way outside, that is.

"You're welcome. Now, are you sure you don't want anything else to take to Robbie and Daisy? A couple of blankets and some tinned fruit doesn't seem enough for what they're going through. I wish I—"

"I know what you wish you could do, but this is more than enough for the moment." Nathan cut Loren off, earning a narrowed eyed stare. "Sorry, Daddy. I don't want you to feel like you need to do more. We've looked after ourselves for many years now. Too much would hinder, not help."

Loren nodded. "You're right. I don't know enough about these things. I'm trusting you to show me the way."

Nathan's mouth widened until he beamed. "Thank you, Daddy." Unable to stop himself, he threw his arms around Loren's neck in a hug he never wanted to end. Loren's arms came around him, holding him tightly against his form.

"Let's get going."

Nathan reluctantly pulled back, wanting to keep hold for longer, but knowing he had things to think about.

They had decided to take a stroll with the shack being close and Nathan feeling better. Nathan decided he needed to speak to Robbie about the situation and get his advice.

Within twenty minutes, they were at the wire fence. Nathan bit his lip again. "You don't have to come—"

"I'm coming," Loren replied, voice firm.

Nathan inhaled deeply then ducked through the hole, holding it open for Loren to get through. Worrying his lips, Nathan led the way around the edge, relaxing minutely as the shack came into view. He hoped they were still there and hadn't moved on. Stopping at the door, he exhaled and knocked twice, opening the door slowly.

Seeing Robbie crouched in front of Daisy, protecting her, had Nathan slumping in relief.

"Nathan!" Daisy pushed Robbie to one side, scrambling up and running to him, throwing her arms around him. "I thought something had happened to you. I'm glad you're alright."

"Hey, Daisy. Yeah, I'm okay. Sorry to worry you."

"What happened to you?" Robbie came forward, frowning, hesitation clear on his face as he inspected Loren up and down. "Nice bruise." He nodded towards Nathan's forehead.

Nathan ran his fingers across the lingering evidence and grimaced. "Yeah, things took a turn for the worse the other night."

"What happened?" Daisy asked, fingers gripping Nathan's coat sleeve.

"Some guy left him injured in an alley. I happened to be walking past and heard him in pain. I helped." Loren filled in the blanks succinctly enough Robbie and Daisy's eyebrows rose.

"What did he do?" Robbie's eyes narrowed, and his lips thinned.

"Doesn't matter. I've been staying with Loren for

the last couple of days to recuperate…" Nathan paused, unsure of how to explain everything.

Robbie tilted his head, locking gazes with Nathan. "You're heading out, aren't you?"

It was what those on the streets called it when someone left the homeless situation.

Nathan bit his lip. "For the moment."

Daisy piped up. "And can you give him what he deserves?" The question was directed at Loren as she manoeuvred around Nathan to stand in front of him.

"I'll give my boy everything he needs."

Robbie and Daisy gasped jointly, redirecting their gazes back to Nathan. He blushed under their perusal. They knew what he wanted from a relationship, so to them, this would be perfect for him. Nathan was unsure because it felt a little like Loren was rescuing him.

He cleared his throat. "Robbie, can I have a word?" He indicated the opposite side of the small space; it wouldn't give them a huge amount of privacy, but enough for what Nathan needed.

Nathan stood with his back to Loren, knowing it would be more difficult if he could see him.

"What's up?"

Running his hand through his hair, he lowered his voice. "I don't know if I'm making a mistake."

Robbie's eyebrows rose again. "Why would you say that?"

Nathan squinted off to one side, focusing inwards instead of outwards. "Am I rushing into this because of how I live my life? On the streets? I can't decide if

I'm…seeing what I want to see instead of what is actually there."

"What's happened between you so far?"

Nathan felt his cheeks flush again. "Nothing sexual." He didn't mention the bathroom scene, it was too embarrassing. "He's taken care of me, took the lead in things we do, cooked for me. Generally taken care of me." He paused, peeking back at Robbie. "He gave me colouring to do while he cooked tonight."

Robbie's mouth curled at the corners. "Grab onto him, Nathan. You'll never know for definite unless you try. We'll be here for you if you need anything." Robbie rubbed the back of his neck, something he did when he was thinking. "Trust yourself. You wouldn't have gone back to his place the other day if you didn't believe he was a good guy, would you?"

Nathan pondered his words and shook his head. "No, I would've told him to piss off."

"Exactly. If the worst comes, come back to us." Robbie reached a hand to Nathan's shoulder, squeezing gently.

"Thanks." Nathan turned, seeing Loren going through the bag they'd brought with them with Daisy. He smiled, turning to his stuff and packing some little bits into a backpack he kept ready for a quick exit. Once he had everything, he pivoted back to Loren. "I'm ready."

Loren nodded, glancing at his friends. "If it eases your concern, Nathan is welcome to leave at any time. He is not being held prisoner, and, although I will try to change his mind, I will never keep him from his freedom." He hesitated. "I put my—our—address in there in case you need anything or want to stop by. You're welcome any time."

Daisy came forward, throwing her arms around Loren, who's eyes widened. Nathan and Robbie guffawed.

As she pulled back, she threw over her shoulder towards Nathan, "He's a keeper."

They said their goodbyes after several more minutes, and Nathan and Loren headed back the way they came.

"I wish I could do more for them." Loren's tone was laced with regret.

"You've done plenty. Giving them a place to come to if they're not safe is one of the best things you could've given them." Nathan sidled up next to Loren and linked his arm around his elbow, resting his head on Loren's shoulder as they ambled back to the house. After a few minutes, Nathan realised what he'd done, and he tensed.

"What's wrong?" Loren asked.

Nathan hesitated. "Nothing. I…I've never felt so at ease with someone as quickly as I have done with you. It's a little unsettling sometimes," he admitted.

"Thank you, Nate."

"For what?" Nathan tilted his head to see Loren's profile.

"For telling me the truth. Where possible, I always want the truth from you, even if you think it will hurt my feelings. Okay?"

"Yes, Daddy," he whispered.

"Good boy."

They continued in silence until they reached Loren's house. Nathan could feel the butterflies beginning in his stomach because he wasn't sure what they were supposed to do tonight.

Loren led the way, helping Nathan out of his coat and shoes then removing his own. Then he held out his hand to Nathan, who grabbed it eagerly.

"Let's go watch TV for a little while before bed."

At the word bed, Nathan pulse skyrocketed, he inhaled and exhaled to slow it. He didn't know what he should be doing. This was new to him, except where he'd had a few interactions with Daddies previously, but nothing to this degree. Those previous meetings had been in a bar and for a release, nothing more.

As they sat, Nathan stared at the TV with fascination, fiddling with his fingers in his lap as Loren found something to watch. The film chosen, Loren sat back, and they watched in silence. Every second that ticked by without conversation, fed Nathan's anxiety.

When a hand rested on his shoulder and pulled him towards Loren with a "Relax, Nate," he went without a fight. Resting his head once more on Loren's shoulder, he tucked his feet under him on the sofa and relaxed into the position.

A gentle shaking motion along with a slide of a hand along his arm woke him gradually. He became aware of a fruity scent and nosed himself further into it, being rewarded with a rumbling chuckle felt through the chest he burrowed into. At the noise, Nathan's eyes opened, instantly taking in his surroundings and finding himself laid on top of Loren on the sofa. He glanced up at Loren, seeing a smirk on his face.

"You were tired, it seemed." Loren's voice was husky, as if he, too, had been asleep, though, Nathan doubted it. Why? He wasn't sure, but he didn't think Loren would've slept while Nathan had.

Nathan pulled back, cheeks flushing with mortification at their positions, which were undoubtedly his fault. "I'm sorry. I didn't mean to fall—"

"Hey, hey. You've nothing to be sorry for." Loren sat up, hands cupping Nathan's jaw and tilting his head until they locked gazes. "You were tired. I loved holding you. You gave me the best gift tonight."

Nathan's brow creased, and he tried to figure out what Loren was trying to say. "I don't—"

"You gave me your trust when you fell asleep on me. You trusted me not to hurt you. You trusted me to keep you safe. That's…" Loren exhaled, "everything."

Nathan checked the truth of his words through his expression. There was a softening in Loren's eyes, a smile on his mouth, and he held Nathan gently.

"Please, Daddy." Nathan wasn't sure exactly what he asked for.

"What do you need, my sweet boy?"

"Could I have a kiss, please, Daddy?" Nathan hadn't known what he wanted until he said the words. Then it was all he wanted. He needed to feel Loren's lips on his. Claiming him. Their first kiss.

Loren's gaze roamed Nathan's face as he smoothed his thumb across Nathan's bottom lip, to which Nathan replied with a quick swipe of his tongue. Loren's gaze darkened, eyes narrowing. He pulled Nathan towards him in infinite slowness. When he got close, Loren went fuzzy, Nathan's eyelashes swept to his cheeks as his breathing increased.

The first press of their lips together was a mere brushing, but when Loren pulled back, Nathan grumbled until Loren returned. The sweet torture continued as Loren pressed kisses across his mouth, jaw and cheeks, returning to his lips and *devoured* Nathan. He could do nothing more than grip the back of Loren's shirt as their lips smashed together, and Loren's tongue explored every inch of Nathan's mouth.

Light-headed but not wanting the kiss to end, Nathan allowed himself to fall deeper into Loren. The movement must have registered because Loren slowed the kiss then pulled back.

Nathan was unable to open his eyes, drunk on passion as he was. He allowed his head to fall back as he struggled to inhale enough air to make him coherent again. When his eyes finally fluttered open, he saw Loren staring at him, lips glistening, eyes shining and mouth grinning.

"You are perfect," his Daddy said.

"Thank you, Daddy."

"Time for bed."

Loren stood, jerking Nathan up by his hands and steadying him when his knees, initially, proved too weak. Once he stood strong, Loren released one hand but kept the other, leading Nathan down the hallway. Outside the spare room, Loren hesitated and turned to him.

"I don't want to assume you are at the same place I am right now. Tonight, you have a choice of where you want to sleep. In the spare room, or with me?"

Nathan rolled his lips, trying to hide his smile. Loren was so considerate. Nathan didn't know why he'd had any reservations about this. "Your room, please, Daddy."

"We're not doing anything else tonight, but I'd love to hold you all night," Loren replied with a pleased expression.

"Yes, Daddy. Please hold me."

"Okay. Do you need anything from the room? Or from your backpack?"

Nathan shook his head.

"Let's get some sleep." They continued down the hallway, Loren opening the door and guiding Nathan to the bed. "Wait here for me."

Nathan stood, fidgeting, gaze roaming the room. He'd been in here earlier in the day but didn't take the time to investigate his surroundings. Instead, he'd gone straight to the drawers to get a t-shirt and found something enticing instead. Nathan smiled, realising his choice that afternoon had led to where he was now, and he couldn't bring himself to regret it. Not that he'd tell his Daddy, of course.

He watched as Loren returned carrying some clothes. "Lift your arms for me, sweetheart." Nathan complied, and Loren removed his t-shirt. "I'm going to change your trousers now." Loren's fingers curled into the waistband of the joggers and slowly nudged them down his legs. "Lift your foot." Nathan rested his hands on Loren's shoulders as he did as he was told. "Other foot."

Once Nathan was naked, Loren reached for the trousers on the bed. He held them out for Nathan to step into and slid the soft, warm fabric up his legs and over his ass. Nathan couldn't help the way his cock jerked, being semi-hard as he was. Loren picked up a top and indicated for Nathan to lift his arms again. Once the pyjama top was in place, Nathan dropped his arms.

"Come on. Jump into bed." Loren reached around him to pull back the duvet, encouraging Nathan to get in and then covering him. "I'm going to get ready. I'll be in after." He pressed a kiss to Nathan's forehead and disappeared into the en-suite.

CHAPTER EIGHT

LOREN

For the first time in a long time, Loren stayed at home to work, content to hear Nathan potter around the house from his vantage point at the kitchen table. He hadn't made a conscious decision to stay home, and he trusted Nathan, but he also wanted to be close to him. He was aware he was not getting as much work done as he would've done if he'd been at the café or the library, and he knew he would have to head there most days; otherwise, he would get behind on his schedule. But he understood himself and knew he needed to be at home that day.

The previous evening had been a revelation. Loren knew Nathan trusted him enough to allow him to stay in his house alone, but he hadn't been sure if Nathan had trusted *him*. He proved the trust last night. Falling asleep on him had turned Loren to tears, and he had been unable to fall asleep alongside him initially, the emotions overwhelming him.

And when Nathan had asked for a kiss, Loren would have done anything to fulfil his wish at that moment.

"Daddy?" A soft voice interrupted his thoughts. He glanced up to see Nathan stood near him, wringing his hands and stepping from foot to foot.

"What do you need, Nate?"

"Would you like a drink?"

Loren tilted his head, scrutinising Nathan as he turned the question over and over in his mind. There was an underlying meaning behind the words, but Loren wasn't sure what they were. Not knowing where Nathan was going with the question had Loren thinking about the correct way to answer.

Being a boy didn't necessarily stop Nathan from doing adult jobs, like helping with meals or making a drink, but Nathan had proved he enjoyed colouring and doing jigsaws, putting him on the lower age limit of being a boy. It was something they had not properly talked about, which Loren would have to rectify that evening.

Taking a chance, he went with his gut instinct. "Yes, please. A cup of tea would be great."

The answering beam was enough of a reply, at least for the moment. Loren watched as Nathan sashayed to the counter, a bounce in his step, settling into his task. He tried to concentrate on the work he'd been completing but found himself watching Nathan's movements instead.

When Nathan turned with a mug in his hand and began drifting towards Loren, his gaze on the mug, Loren saw the tip of his tongue peek out between his lips in concentration. He grinned and thanked Nathan when it was placed next to him.

"You're welcome, Daddy." Nathan twisted to leave the room, but Loren called him back. "Yes, Daddy?"

"Come here, sweet boy."

Nathan returned to him without hesitation, and his heart felt full to bursting.

"I'd love to reward you." Loren crooked a finger at Nathan, enticing him to come closer, which Nathan did. Loren reached a hand up to Nathan's neck and pulled him in for a kiss. As their lips touched, Loren felt a fire begin in the pit of his stomach, which flamed higher when Nathan moaned into his mouth. Keeping it chaste was hard work, but Loren pulled away after a few minutes, keeping hold of Nathan's neck until he opened his eyes and regained his balance.

"Thank you, Daddy," Nathan whispered.

"You're welcome. Now, go have fun while I get some more work done."

Nathan grinned. "I will, Daddy." He skipped to the doorway, pausing when Loren called his name again.

"You don't have to call me Daddy all the time if you don't want to, you know." Loren had been curious about that since Nathan had started saying the word; it seemed to be in every sentence he spoke. He didn't want Nathan to think he had to call him Daddy in every interaction. Loren watched as a flush tinted

Nathan's cheeks as he ducked his head and mumbled his response. "I didn't hear you, Nate."

Nathan inhaled and peered at Loren. "I love saying it, Daddy."

Loren's mouth curled up. "Okay, then."

Nathan beamed and exited the kitchen. A few minutes later, Loren heard the TV, and he relaxed back into his seat. He was concerned Nathan accepted their…relationship…because Loren had helped him, and he didn't want that to be the reason.

Turning back to his accounts, Loren got to work, promising himself they would have a discussion after their meal that evening.

<—————————>

Loren stirred the chicken together with the sauce, mentally creating bullet points of the things he needed to talk to Nathan about, a conversation they should have had yesterday. It wasn't a conversation he'd had more than a few times so trying to cover everything was pointless, and some of it they would have to work out as they went along. If Nathan decided to stay. And there was the crux of the matter. Loren wanted Nathan to stay and be his boy, but he needed Nathan to want to stay.

He recalled his earlier conversation with Ben on the phone. Loren had called him to tell him about having found his boy, and, while they were overjoyed about it, Ben cautioned him about jumping in with both feet. He understood Ben's reservations, but Loren needed to speak to Nathan before anything was agreed.

"Nate?"

A few seconds later, Nathan poked his head through the kitchen doorway. "Yes, Daddy?"

"Could you set the table, please?"

Nathan, wearing the same clothes Loren had dressed him in that morning, reached up for the plates and glasses and placed them on the table, then returned for cutlery.

Loren emptied the pan contents into a serving bowl and carried it to the table. "Thank you, Nate. Enjoy your food." Loren spooned some of the chicken pasta onto Nathan's plate, passing it to him, offering him the salad bowl as well.

"This looks and smells delicious. Thank you, Daddy."

"You're welcome. Eat up."

Loren watched as Nathan picked up his fork and speared pieces of chicken and pasta onto it, placing it in his mouth, pulling the tines out again and licking his lips before chewing with a puckered brow. Loren didn't interrupt his musings. If Nathan had questions, Loren wanted him to ask when he was ready.

They ate in silence—comfortable silence—until Nathan had finished his plate. Seemingly snapping out of a daze, Nathan glanced to Loren, eyes wide.

"What's wrong?"

"I'm sorry, Daddy!" Nathan spoke in a rush as he dropped his fork to the table.

"Calm down, Nathan. What are you sorry about?" Loren reached a hand forward and covered Nathan's trembling one.

"I've not spoken to you since we sat. I didn't mean to be so quiet. I was thinking about everything that has happened since I met you, and I thought about Robbie and Daisy and the things I had to do…previously. I didn't realise how long I'd been thinking until I saw my plate was empty. I didn't mean to ignore you. I would never do—"

Loren stood, halting Nathan's words, crouching next to Nathan's chair. "Shhh, sweet boy. Calm down. Take a breath for me, okay? Breathe, that's it." Loren rubbed a circle on Nathan's back while holding a hand over both of Nathan's in his lap. "Right, one more. That's it." He waited until Nathan had followed the instruction. "Have you finished your dinner?" Nathan nodded, eyes downcast. "Okay. Let's sit on the sofa and talk for a while, alright, sweetheart?"

Loren pulled him to standing, and, not letting go of his hand, led him to the sofa where he sat and pulled Nathan onto his lap. At first, Nathan sat upright until Loren placed a hand on his back again and tugged him closer.

"Right, now. Let's have a chat." Nathan tensed in his arms again, and although Nathan was snuggled under his chin, Loren knew he was about to apologise again. "You have nothing to apologise for," Loren cut in before Nathan could say a word. "You don't have to talk if you don't want to. I have lived most of my life without someone to chat at the kitchen table. It's not a new scenario for me. You don't need to worry about offending me. I will say, however, if there is something you want to talk to me about or something you are worried about, I would love it if you could share it with me. I fully believe in 'a problem shared is a problem halved,' but," he continued, rubbing Nathan's back again, "you don't *have* to. My role as your Daddy is to look after your wellbeing, but also, to be there when you need someone. Do you understand what I'm trying to say?"

There was silence for a few seconds, then Nathan nodded against Loren's chest. "I think I understand, Daddy."

"Good. We need to talk through a few things, and there's no better time than now. Sit up for me, Nate." Loren helped Nathan rise from his position and sat him right next to him so he could see Nathan's face. "I know you told me a little about what you wanted yesterday. Is there anything else you want from this relationship, Nathan?"

Loren watched emotions fly across Nathan's face, then Nathan's gaze dropped to the floor; he was pleased Nathan considered his answer, rather than automatically replying.

"I would like someone to take care of me and to help me figure out how to take care of myself properly. I would like an emotional connection with someone. And to have hugs and cuddles whenever I want them."

Smiling, Loren cupped Nathan's jaw. "I would love to be that person for you."

Nathan's gaze locked to his as he whispered, "I would love that person to be you."

Loren leaned in, placing a chaste kiss to Nathan's lips. "There are many things we need to discuss. For example, what do you want to happen about sex?"

Nathan blushed and ducked his head again. "I…I would like to have sex with you. I want you to give me what you think I need, Daddy. I don't have experience of emotional sex, only…" Nathan trailed off, waving a hand around.

"I understand. We can figure it out together, how about that? And we will both get tested, so you know I'm safe."

Nathan ducked his head. "And to check if I am, too, Daddy."

"We'll check us both, so we know we are both safe." He paused. "You seem to be content with the 'Daddy' word since we started this. What do you want to do about our dynamic when we go out in public?" Loren had no preferences either way when it came to his public persona.

Cocking his head, Nathan bit his lip. "I think I would like to keep calling you Daddy. But…can we see when we do it? If it doesn't feel comfortable, I won't say it."

"That's fine, Nate. Thank you for taking the time to answer honestly."

"What would you like me to do as your boy, Daddy?" Nathan stared at him with such openness and curiosity.

"I want you to be yourself. I don't want you to

change who you are for me. This will only work if we are honest with each other."

"And what happens if I do something I shouldn't?" Nathan bit his lip again, something Loren would need to curb him of; he hated the idea Nathan was hurting himself.

"Well, that is something we need to decide upon. We can have certain boundaries you need to work within or certain tasks, which need to be undertaken to make sure you are healthy and strong. And if your behaviour needs to be corrected, I will think of appropriate punishment."

Loren heard an audible intake of breath and chuckled. His boy liked the idea of punishment, it seemed. He knew it wouldn't take long for Nathan's behaviour to *challenge* the boundaries, whatever they may be.

"Okay, Daddy."

"Good boy." Lifting his hand to cup Nathan's jaw again, he pulled him closer. "I think it's time we sealed the deal."

Their lips met in a sweet caress until Nathan groaned, and Loren dragged Nathan across his lap, deepening the kiss. Nathan wrapped his arms around Loren's neck, straddling him properly. Loren slid his tongue along the roof of Nathan's mouth, gripping the back of his head, and moving him where Loren wanted him, Nathan providing a background noise of moans and groans.

Running a hand down Nathan's back, Loren teased his fingers into the top of the waistband of his trousers, pawing at the top of his ass cheeks, letting one finger stray to the tip of his crack. Nathan arched his ass back towards Loren's hands.

"That's what you want, is it, sweet boy? Hmm? You'll have to be good to get it, won't you?" Loren didn't expect any answer to be forthcoming with the haze covering Nathan's expression. Sliding his finger closer to Nathan's hole, Loren licked a strip up Nathan's neck, sucking a bruise under his jaw, marking him for all to see. A little caveman mentality there, but he couldn't resist.

At Nathan's next needy groan, Loren pulled away gently, taking Nathan's chin into his hand to focus his attention. "Let's head to bed." Not planning on sealing the deal tonight, Loren lifted Nathan off his lap, grabbed his hand and dragged him up the stairs to the bedroom, straight into the en-suite. "Shower time, sweetheart."

After helping Nathan out of his clothes and switching on the shower, Loren indicated for Nathan to get in. When Nathan hesitated, he asked if something was wrong.

Nathan bit his lip and stared to one side. "Can you shower with me, please, Daddy?"

Loren reached forward, running his fingers through Nathan's hair. "Of course. You jump in. I don't want you getting cold. I'll join you in a moment."

Nodding, Nathan did as instructed. Loren had the best of intentions of not doing anything else that night, but it appeared as if something would happen, after all. There was no way he would be able to deny the boy, especially with how good he was being. A reward was in order.

He removed his clothes, throwing them into the hamper by the door and sliding into the shower behind Nathan, who stepped back into him and rested his head on Loren's shoulder. Loren stroked his hands across Nathan's wet skin, teasing his nipples, and the needy sounds escaping from Nathan, hardening his cock more than it already was.

Their heights, as they were, enabled Loren to rest his swollen cock against the crack of Nathan's ass. Every time the boy arched into the fingers teasing his nipples, his ass pressed harder against Loren's shaft.

There was no way Loren would last long in this scenario. As he went to change their positions, Nathan mouthed at his ear, "Please, can I suck your cock, Daddy?"

Loren let out a shaky breath and swallowed. Hard. "You ask so nicely, sweet boy, and you have been good for me. Yes, you can."

He watched as a delighted expression crossed Nathan's face, and he immediately whirled around to face Loren and dropped to his knees. When water sprayed onto his face, Loren pulled Nathan up again, smiling. He reversed their positions, the water pounded against his back, sheltering Nathan.

Nathan kneeled at his feet, his big doe eyes peering up at Loren as if he was as innocent as they come. A good disguise, but Loren had already seen behind the expression and knew Nathan could be a brat if he wasn't trying so hard to please. Time would tell.

Nathan ran his hands up Loren's legs, both surrounding the base of his cock at their finishing position. Using one hand, Nathan encircled the purple shaft, pulling it to his mouth, where he licked the tip repeatedly, teasing the slit. Minutes, or seconds, later, Nathan wrapped his lips around the head, using his tongue to drive Loren crazy, alternating between the tip and the nerves under the crown of his dick. Loren felt every swipe of the talented tongue as small electrical shocks filtered through his system. He tried his hardest not to grab hold of Nathan and keep him where he wanted him. This was Nathan's time for exploring. But Nathan had other ideas. He grabbed Loren's hands, guiding them to his hair, pushing against them as he took Loren's weeping dick further into his mouth.

Loren got the idea. He gripped Nathan's head in his hands and pulled him forward, sinking further into the warm, wet mouth before pulling away again. He was conscious of not going too far in and choking Nathan. He repeated the action several times and he felt a vibration on his cock, making his eyes roll back in his head. When he guided Nathan back down once more, Nathan pulled away from his hands and sank Loren's shaft straight down his throat and swallowed.

"Fuck!" Loren lost it. After that manoeuvre, Loren had no control, he fucked Nathan's mouth and throat, then blew his load, barely warning Nathan. Never had he ever lost control like that. With anyone. He rested against the tiled wall, catching his breath, watching Nathan rise from under lowered eyelids.

"Was it okay?"

Loren snorted. "Fuck, yes, Nate. It was…" He couldn't finish. He could barely think. Wrapping his boy in his arms, they stayed locked together while Loren recuperated. When Nathan shivered, he turned Nathan back into the stream of the shower, facing forward. It was time he rewarded his boy.

Sliding his hand down Nathan's abs and gripping his cock, his other hand reached further down to play with his balls and synchronising his movements with Nathan's answering groans, he quickly had Nathan on the edge.

"Please, Daddy!"

"What do you want, Nate?" Loren knew exactly what he craved, but he wanted Nathan to ask for it. He wanted Nathan to wait until *Daddy* said he could come.

"Please! Can I come, Daddy? Please, can I come?" Nathan's fingernails were embedded in Loren's forearms, his head resting back against Loren's shoulder as his hips thrust in time with Loren's motions. "Please, Daddy?"

Loren waited for a beat more and replied, "Come for me, my sweet boy." He hadn't finished his words when Nathan's release painted the tiles, his groans loud in Loren's ear but musical all the same.

When Nathan's knees refused to keep him upright, Loren banded an arm around his waist and proceeded to wash him with infinite care in the now-lukewarm water. Switching off the shower, Loren managed to dry Nathan off partially and danced him towards the bed. Flicking the cover to the side, he helped Nathan to lay down and pulled the cover back over him. Loren leaned down to kiss his forehead, wishing him a good sleep.

He finished drying himself, checked everything was locked up properly and strode back to his bed…and his boy, tucking up tight against Nathan's back.

CHAPTER NINE

NATHAN

Nathan wandered around the empty house, wanting to search from top to bottom to see what he could find out about Loren. But, although Loren had said to treat the house as his own, Nathan couldn't do it. It wasn't his home; he was staying there for a short time.

That morning, before Loren had left for the library, he had woken Nathan with sweet kisses along his neck, cheeks and mouth.

"Good morning, sweet boy. Did you sleep well?" Loren braced himself on his elbow, tracing Nathan's stomach with his free hand.

Nathan's mouth curled in a content smile. "Yes, thank you, Daddy. Our bed is comfy." He snuggled his head into the pillow and closer to Loren's naked chest, taking a deep breath.

"I'm glad you think so. I am going to spend the day at the

*library today. I have a bit of work to complete by the end of the
week."*

*Nathan opened his eyes, blinking sleepily. "What should
I do?"*

*"You can do whatever you'd like to do, Nate. Make yourself
at home." Loren kissed his nose. "What would you like for
breakfast? Pancakes? Toast?"*

Biting his lips, Nathan replied, "Pancakes, please, Daddy."

"Pancakes, it is."

*Nathan reached up a hand to cup Loren's cheek but hesitated
before he made contact. Loren covered the hand and pressed it to
his cheek, turning to kiss Nathan's palm, the scratchy stubble tickling the sensitive skin.*

"Are you okay?"

*Nathan's gaze roamed the expanse of Loren's face, noticing
the dips and valleys in his skin and loving every one of them.
Loving? What was he thinking? He cleared his throat. "Yes,
Daddy. I'm okay."*

*"Good." Loren leaned down and kissed Nathan once more.
"Let me get breakfast done, and we'll shower and get you dressed
for the day."*

After circuiting the house once more, he decided to
go and visit Robbie and Daisy again. Not wanting to
ruin his new clothes, he re-dressed in his old street
clothes, as he called them now, and packed a few pieces
of fruit and a couple of yoghurts, along with some
tinned meat, into his backpack and, grabbing the spare
set of keys from where Loren had pointed them out, he
locked the house and drifted down the road.

He did have a small amount of money in his
pocket, but he didn't want to waste it on a taxi; there-

fore, he took a meandering stroll, watching as the houses changed to shops, then to high-rises. In no time, he was at the fence, cutting his way across the open space and knocking on the door in the pattern they had all agreed on.

Daisy opened the door hesitantly, beaming when she saw him, making him feel settled once more.

She pulled the door wider. "Come on in. Why didn't you come in? You know you're always welcome here."

"I wasn't sure if you two had planned to find somewhere else to stay. I didn't want to intrude on someone else." Nathan glanced around. "Where's Robbie?"

Daisy went back to her blanket, sitting against the wall. "He went to see if there were any job openings listed at the shelter."

Nathan raised his eyebrows. "I thought he didn't want to?" He made himself comfortable on the floor, stretching his legs out in front of him and setting the backpack down.

Daisy stared at her hands, rubbing them together in slow motion. "He doesn't, but…"

Nathan frowned when Daisy stopped talking. His stomach cramped. "Daisy? What's wrong? Why is Robbie searching for work when you both have been vocal about being happy as you are?" His breathing came faster. His thoughts were on the worst scenarios, one being Daisy was ill, and they needed the money for medical expenses. Surely, they would ask him for help if they needed something. He was in a better position to help them now, and he would be able to get a job himself to help pay for it.

Daisy peered up at him, tears in her eyes, a small smile on her face. "I'm pregnant," she whispered.

Nathan stared at her, mouth flapping. All of the difficulties they were about to face ran through his mind. He could now understand why Robbie was out looking for a job. "Wow. Congratulations?" He said the word as a question because, although he'd seen her contentment, he wasn't sure if it was something they were happy about or not.

Daisy snickered. "Yes, thanks. It's a happy thing. Unexpected but happy."

Nathan moved over next to Daisy and wrapped an arm around her shoulder. Kissing the side of her head, he murmured, "You'll be great parents."

"Thanks, Nathan."

"Have you talked about what you plan to do?"

"A little. Enough that Robbie is job hunting. We're not sure what the plans about housing are yet. We need to speak with the shelter and see if they have any ideas of what we could do and where we could go. But it's little yet; we have a bit of time to sort things out."

Nathan squeezed her shoulders and rested his head on top of hers.

They stayed in that position for a short time until Nathan remembered what he'd brought with him. "I come bearing gifts." He reached for his bag, pulling out the food and showing Daisy.

She pressed her nose against the oranges and inhaled, eyes closing. She held the oranges as if they were precious, which, in some ways, they were. "Thanks, Nathan," she repeated. Still holding the fruit, she settled back against the wall again as Nathan placed the other items on the small box next to him. "How are things with Loren?"

"Good. I think."

"What do you mean, you think? Is he hurting you?" She sat upright, eyes narrowed.

"Hold fire, mama-bear." Nathan snorted at her automatic defensive stand. "No, he's not hurting me. It's…a lot to get used to. I've been on the streets for so long, it's difficult to get comfortable somewhere where it can all be taken away again. I wonder whether I should stay on the streets, then I won't have to worry about it every minute of the day."

He felt awful saying these things. He knew Loren wouldn't throw him out, even if their relationship didn't work, but it was difficult to remove those thoughts from his head. On the streets, he had to work for everything he needed, and he only owned a few things. If they had been taken from him, all he would have to do is *work* to be able to get them again. Whereas staying with Loren in comfort made him forget how difficult living on the streets was…and he didn't think it was a good thing.

"Oh, Nathan. I could tell Loren feels deeply for you. I don't think you have to worry about it all crashing down around you. And I can see you care for him." She paused. "Does he give you what you need? Emotionally, I mean?"

Nathan's smile grew. "Yeah, he's amazing."

"More information than I needed!" Daisy pretended to block her ears.

Swatting at her, he laughed. "No, I don't mean that way. We've not…" he stopped, examining the floor.

Daisy turned towards him, crossing her legs, holding the oranges on her lap. "You've not had sex yet?"

"No. Well, technically, yes, if you call a blowjob sex. But not…all the way." Nathan's cheeks warmed under Daisy's scrutiny.

She snorted. "I can't believe you're blushing when we're talking about sex! Who are you?"

"Shut up!" He pushed against her shoulder in mock irritation, then they both burst out laughing.

"What's all this noise?"

Nathan's gaze swung to the door, heart in his throat at the possibility of their shelter being taken away from them, but his shoulders sagged when he saw Robbie. "If it wouldn't be a waste of food, I would throw this fruit at you, asshole! You scared the shit out of me."

Robbie laughed. "Serves you right, pushing my girlfriend like that." He shut the door behind him, dropping his bag near the entrance and hurrying over to Daisy, planting a kiss on her lips. "Hey, sweetheart, how are you feeling?"

Daisy blushed, ducking her chin. "I'm good." She held up the oranges. "Nathan brought vitamin C."

Robbie glanced at him with a grin. "Thanks, man."

"I hear congratulations is in order?" Nathan smirked.

Robbie beamed, a light shining brighter in his eyes. "Thanks." He dropped to a seated position next to Daisy, linking their fingers. "What brings you out here, anyway? Not that we mind the company."

"He was asking for sex advice," Daisy said with a straight face.

Robbie's mouth gaped, eyebrows raised. "What?"

"Shut up, Daisy! No, I wasn't. You started it." Nathan pouted, crossing his arms over his chest.

Daisy and Robbie cracked up, and Nathan rolled his eyes, joining in.

When they regained their breath, Nathan explained, "I didn't specifically ask for advice. I was saying, Loren and I hadn't had sex yet if you didn't include a blowjob as sex."

"Why haven't you slept with him?"

"It's not for lack of wanting to, Robbie! God!" Nathan snorted, then continued quieter, "You know who he is to me. He's taking it slowly. Not wanting to take advantage of the situation. And we're waiting for test results, too. I want to be sure I'm not...Anyway, it's...great."

Robbie cocked his head. "You want him to ravish you."

The deadpan tone hit the nail on the head. "Yes! My feelings are all mixed up. I feel cared for but also unsure and, in some ways, unwanted. Mainly the latter when he's not around. Maybe it's my issue and nothing to do with him."

"I disagree," Daisy said. "It has everything to do with him. He needs to make sure he takes care of you when he's not around as well. It's part of his job. And he should know that."

"Has he punished you yet?" Robbie smirked.

Nathan chuckled. "No."

"How come?" Robbie frowned.

"I've been a good boy." Nathan leered.

"Doesn't sound like you. What's stopping you from being yourself, apart from being unsure?"

Nathan hesitated, biting his lip. He loved being a good boy for Loren. The attention he received was amazing, but…something was missing.

"You don't want to take things too far and risk him throwing you away?"

Once more, Daisy hit it spot on. Nathan nodded.

"He wouldn't, you know." Daisy wrapped her arm around his shoulders.

"You need to speak to him about it. You both need to be on the same page. Is he waiting for you to get home?"

Nathan shook his head, clearing his throat. "No, he went to work at the library today, as he usually does. I felt weird staying there by myself, so I came to see you."

Robbie's eyebrows rose as the corners of his mouth turned up. "Did you tell him where you were going?"

"No. I don't have a phone to message him on, do I?" Nathan frowned, not understanding what Robbie's expression was about.

"You didn't think to leave a note on the table or something?"

Nathan's eyes widened, he scrambled to his feet.

"Shit. I best get back. Loren doesn't usually finish work until around four, I have time."

"Nathan, calm down. I think you did this as a test. You knew exactly what you were doing when you left. Even if you didn't realise it at the time."

He paused what he was doing and stared at Robbie, brow creased. "What do you mean?"

"Well, you said you've not had sex yet. You also said you're not sure how you feel about everything, and you said you have yet to be punished." Robbie paused and sighed when no one said anything. "I think you are trying to provoke a reaction from Loren."

"No! I…I'm not used to…I didn't think…fuck!" Nathan sat back, his hands gripping his hair. He closed his eyes and calmed his breathing, examining his earlier thoughts when he was at the house. Yes, he had been all turned around and hadn't known what to do with himself, but did he want to be punished?

He worried his bottom lip as he thought through everything. His shoulders sagged, and his head rested back against the wall, hands dropping into his lap. "You're right. I didn't realise it at the time, but I was annoyed at Loren for leaving me alone without any idea of what I should be doing. He told me to treat the house as my own, but I have no idea what I enjoy doing anymore. The idea of leaving a note did briefly cross my mind, but I believed I'd be home before he was." He sighed.

"What are you planning on doing now you've realised what you want?" Daisy asked.

Nathan stared at the roof of the shelter, feeling the

cool breeze from one of the gaps in the wooden shack as he considered his options. It was unlikely Loren would be home before Nathan, but if he was, did it matter whether Nathan was home earlier...or later? He'd still get punished.

"I'm planning on hanging out with my friends for a while longer, then I'll head home." He rolled his head towards them, a smirk crossing his face. "May as well make the punishment worthwhile."

They all laughed at Nathan's answer, who, despite his words, was unsure if it was the correct course of action. He guessed he'd see when he returned.

CHAPTER
TEN

LOREN

Loren entered the house to complete stillness, a complete and utter lack of presence, and he knew instinctively Nathan wasn't there.

He closed the door behind him, wandering to the kitchen table to drop his bag and keys. Glancing around, he studied the kitchen, seeing nothing out of place. He continued his perusal through the rest of the downstairs, climbing the stairs, a lump in his throat, making it difficult to breathe. He checked the bathroom first, then their bedroom, and when he saw nothing to indicate anyone was here, he trudged towards the spare room.

The door was closed, and Loren stood in front of it, pulse skyrocketing, sweat gathering at the base of his spine. He didn't know what he wished for: Nathan to be in there or not. If he was, Loren was unsure why he'd prefer the spare room to their bedroom. If he wasn't, he had no idea where Nathan would be.

Heart pounding, Loren turned the handle and pushed the door open. Standing at the threshold, he saw no one. Shoulders sagging, he caught himself on the doorframe, breathing deeply and stumbling towards the bed, where he fell to his knees in front of the clothes he had dressed Nathan in that morning.

The clothes were thrown haphazardly across the bed as if Nathan had been in a rush. Loren scanned the room for Nathan's street clothes and his backpack, and, seeing neither, he turned and sat on the floor by the bed.

Stretching his legs out in front, he dropped his hands to his lap and rested his head back, staring at the ceiling. As tears rolled into his hairline, he tried to understand what he'd done wrong. When he'd left this morning, Nathan had been smiling and seemingly happy. There was nothing to indicate Nathan had wanted to leave him. Lifting his head, he bent his knees, crossing his arms across the top and resting his forehead on them.

He had no idea how long he'd sat there, or how many tears he had cried when he heard the front door open. Staying in the same position, he ignored it, thinking he imagined things. It was only when he heard footsteps mounting the stairs that his heart began hammering once more.

"Loren?" The voice was quiet but clear and coming from the doorway. "Loren? Is everything okay?"

Loren lifted his tear-stained face to the doorway, not knowing whether to believe the apparition or not.

"Loren?" Nathan stepped further into the room.

With that movement, Loren sprang up from the floor and flew towards Nathan, enfolding him in his arms and tucking his face into Nathan's neck. As Nathan's arms came around him, Loren lost it. They stood in the embrace for several minutes before Loren became aware of Nathan rubbing a hand up and down his back and speaking.

"I'm sorry, Daddy. So sorry. I should've left you a note. I didn't think things through. I'm sorry," Nathan repeated the words over and over again.

Loren inhaled, opened his eyes and pulled back. Cupping Nathan's jaw, he gazed into the apologetic chestnut-brown eyes. "You will be punished for this bad behaviour, boy." He felt Nathan swallow. "But later. I need you too much, right now." Lips met in a fierce clash as Loren took what he needed from Nathan. Nathan's hand went from stroking his back to gripping his shirt, little moans sounding from the back of his throat while Loren unleashed his frantic need. The overwhelming pressure of holding back was now being released, and Nathan stood in the centre of it.

Loren strode forward, making Nathan stumble back as he clung to Loren as he directed them to their bedroom, all the while kissing Nathan until he was lightheaded. When Nathan stumbled again, Loren gripped the back of his thighs and lifted his legs to wrap around Loren's waist. Nathan changed his grasp, encircling his arms around Loren's head. Opening his eyes partially to see where they were in the hallway, Loren stomped towards the bedroom door, which, thankfully, was open from his earlier search.

Pausing at the side of the bed, Loren lowered Nathan to the floor, ripping his mouth away and gasping for breath. They stood staring, hands holding each other. Loren lifted a hand and rubbed at the bruised, wet lips gracing Nathan's face. Nathan's eyelids lowered, and he licked at Loren's finger.

"Let's get you undressed." Sliding his hand down the column of Nathan's neck, he pushed the jacket off his shoulders, allowing it to drop heavily to the floor, then found the hem of his t-shirt, pulling it up and over Nathan's head and threw it down. Nathan's eyebrows rose as he glanced between the discarded t-shirt and Loren. Smirking, Loren leaned in for another kiss, distracting Nathan from whatever thoughts were going through his head. A shiver went through Nathan's body, breaking Loren from their kiss. "Lay down, sweetheart."

Watching as Nathan obeyed, Loren began undressing, dropping his clothes to the floor. He kept his boxers on and crawled on all fours to Nathan's prone body. Stopping next to him, Loren ran a hand from Nathan's waistband to his navel, up his abs to his chest, bypassing the nubs seeking attention. Continuing to slide his hand upwards, he cupped Nathan's jaw, leaning on his elbow to sip at the swollen lips.

"Are you okay, Nathan?" Loren whispered against his mouth. Nathan nodded. "I need words, my boy."

Clearing his throat, Nathan uttered, "Yes, Daddy."

"We can stop anytime, just say the word, alright?"

"Please, don't stop, Daddy." Nathan closed his eyes, a bodily shiver running through him again when Loren grazed a nipple. "Please, don't stop."

Loren grinned. "As you wish." He replaced his fingers with his mouth, using the firm tip of his tongue to lash at the erect nub and watching as Nathan's hands fisted the sheets below. Nathan's voice rose when Loren's hand found his other nipple, giving it a similar treatment.

"Daddy!"

Loren's free hand slid to the button of Nathan's trousers, undoing it and relieving some pressure on Nathan's cock. Removing his hand from Nathan's nipple, he tucked both hands into the sides of Nathan's trousers, pushing them down as Loren's mouth moved to the opposite nub. When he couldn't push them any further, his mouth left the sensitive peak and kissed down Nathan's abs where the trousers were pulled off, the underwear closely following, and thrown in the vicinity of the rest.

From his position, it was difficult to miss Nathan's erect cock, standing proud. Eyes locked onto Nathan's face, Loren slowly pushed Nathan's legs apart, revelling in the pupil-blown expression. "I'm going to take care of you, now, Nate." He removed his boxers and crawled in between Nathan's spread legs after reaching for the items from the bedside table.

Sliding his hands up Nathan's shins, knees and thighs, Loren marvelled at the smoothness of his skin until his gaze was caught on his weeping shaft.

"You're beautiful, Nate."

"Thank you, Daddy," Nathan choked, arousal lowering his voice.

Loren situated himself on his stomach, his face close to the swollen cock. Unable to resist, Loren licked a strip up the shaft, earning a groan from Nathan, enticing Loren to do it again, finishing with a swipe of his tongue to collect the precome. He grabbed the lube he'd retrieved and squeezed some onto his fingers, making sure to keep Nathan's focus on his cock. Rubbing around his hole, Loren sucked the head of Nathan's cock, swallowing him down as Loren breached him.

"Yes! More, Daddy!"

From his position, Loren could see Nathan's head pressed back into the pillow, fists still clenched in the sheets. Loren lifted and lowered his head on the swollen shaft as he prepared Nathan's ass. They had not spoken about what Nathan preferred, but Loren was unwilling to take him without the proper preparation, no matter how much of a rush he was in to claim his boy.

When Nathan could take three fingers, Loren deemed him ready, especially with the incoherent noises Nathan was making. Loren released Nathan's cock and lifted to his knees, grabbed the condom, rolled it on and slicked it.

Loren leaned his hands either side of Nathan's torso and brought their faces close together. "Look at me, sweet boy." He gazed at the sheen of sweat coating Nathan's skin and similarly at the blissed expression when those eyes met his. "Are you ready for me?"

"Yes, please, Daddy. Make me yours," Nathan breathed.

Loren's heart soared at the words, and he dipped down to kiss those delectable lips. "As you wish." Kneeling back again, he pushed Nathan's legs further apart, and bracing one hand on the bed and one holding his cock, he pressed forward against Nathan's hole.

Unable to decide where to look, Loren flicked his gaze between where his cock was and Nathan's face, watching every nuance of muscle movement for pain. When he saw nothing except pleasure, he surged forward, claiming every inch of Nathan he could.

"Fuck, Nate, you feel amazing." Staying fully inside of Nathan, Loren lowered to his elbows, covering Nathan's body, getting as close as he could. "Wrap your arms around me, Nate."

Nathan blinked his eyes up at Loren, then complied, sliding them around his neck and one hand into Loren's hair. Loren closed the distance between their lips, unable to resist, and as they explored, he began to move his hips in a slow, torturous rhythm.

Loren could feel Nathan's hard cock rubbing between their stomachs, and by the twitching in the stomach muscles, he knew Nathan wouldn't last long. He slid his arms underneath Nathan's back, one hand resting against his shoulder, the other gripping his ass cheeks, holding him close and tilting him exactly right. He thrust his hips harder.

"Oh my god! Oh! Please, Daddy." Nathan's moans escaped when he tore his mouth from Loren's and arched his head back. "Right there! Oh, please, Daddy! Can I come? Please!"

Nibbling at the muscle straining between his shoulder and neck, Loren increased his speed. "Fuck! Yes, Nate! Come! Now!"

With the order, Nathan's body seized, the rhythmic clenching on Loren's cock blinding him with his orgasm.

Loren rested his weight on his arms once more so Nathan could breathe but stayed plastered against him, inhaling his sweaty, sex-scented smell. After a few minutes, he lifted his head, smiling when he saw Nathan with his eyes closed, mouth open and a gorgeous flush to his skin. Loren pressed a kiss to his collarbone and rose off him, laughing when Nathan's arms flopped to the bed.

"Come on, sweetheart. It's time for a bath."

"Mmm," was the response he received.

Chuckling, he strode to the en-suite and cleaned himself off before plugging the bath and turning on the taps. Throwing in some relaxing salts, he returned to the bedroom, shaking his head when he found Nathan in the same position.

"You'll get sore if you stay in that position all night. Let me help you up." He placed one knee on the bed and slid his hands under Nathan's knees and shoulders, lifting him with ease. Manoeuvring Nathan through the door and into the tub was easy...waking him up was not. "Come on, Nate, wake a little, so I can wash you properly without you drowning." With one arm wrapped under his shoulders to keep him from sinking, Loren grabbed a sponge and soap and lathered it, gently stroking it across Nathan's skin. Loren shook his head again when there was no response other than a small sniffle.

Giving up, Loren forewent washing Nathan's hair and scrubbed his body clean as best he could. Popping the plug out, the bathwater emptied as he grabbed a towel and pulled Nathan to a semi-sitting position. Having to bear the brunt of his, albeit light, weight, Loren rested the towel over the top of Nathan and grabbed another, doing the same. Lifting him from the bath, Loren strode back to the bed, crouching to spread a towel on the sheets, laying Nathan on it, and placing another towel over the top.

Loren snorted at the sight. Nathan had to be fast asleep; otherwise, there was no way he would've slept through everything. Loren should take it as a compliment, perhaps.

He dried Nathan off as best he could under the circumstances, pulling the towel from underneath him when he was done, then tucked the covers around him. Returning to the bathroom, he tidied up in there, then switched off the light and picked up the clothes from the floor of the bedroom. He didn't want Nathan tripping over them in the middle of the night. Checking the house was locked up, he returned to the bed and slid in behind Nathan, curling himself around him tightly.

Inhaling Nathan's sweet scent, Loren held him a

little tighter, remembering what had happened earlier. He had been certain Nathan had left and wouldn't be coming back. When Nathan had appeared in the doorway, Loren had been relieved, he hadn't considered a punishment. At least until a little anger had shown up. Tomorrow would be the test of their relationship, if Nathan wanted a relationship. Their first conversation the next morning would be about their expectations, then, and only then, will they discuss the need for Nathan to be punished for what he had put Loren through. After all, although they had not specified what they were doing, Nathan should have thought about the consequences of him leaving without mentioning where he was going.

Loren frowned. Should he expect Nathan to tell him where he is every minute of the day? Ideally, yes. It's what the Daddy in him needed. But could he punish Nathan when it hadn't been discussed before it happened? Loren wasn't sure.

Nathan moved in his sleep, snuggling deeper into Loren's embrace. He didn't want to risk scaring Nathan away. But he also had to put everything on the line to explain what he needed from a relationship. And he didn't know what he would do if Nathan turned and walked away.

←————————————→

Leaving Nathan warm and content in their bed that morning had been excruciating, but Loren wanted to cook Nathan a rejuvenating breakfast and ready him for the conversation to come.

"Daddy?" Nathan's sleepy voice broke into Loren's musings, and he twisted towards the doorway to find his boy dressed in joggers and a large t-shirt—one of his.

"Good morning, sweet boy. Did you sleep well?" He drifted over to kiss Nathan on the side of his head, his cheek and, finally, his mouth.

A rush of red filled Nathan's cheeks as he nodded. "Yes, thank you, Daddy."

"Good. Sit. Let's get some breakfast inside you." Loren shared out the cooked breakfast he'd made and placed a plate in front of Nathan, whose eyes widened.

"Wow. That is a lot of food, Daddy."

Loren chuckled. "Don't worry if you can't eat it all, Nate. Eat what you can. I wasn't sure how hungry you would be this morning."

"Thank you, Daddy." Nathan picked up his fork and began shovelling the contents into his mouth, moaning with every bite.

Snorting, Loren chided, "Not so fast, Nate. The food isn't going anywhere." Nathan ducked his head and slowed his chewing, apologising when his mouth was empty. "It's okay. I don't want you getting a poorly stomach later."

They ate in comfortable silence, locking gazes often, swapping smiles and small caresses. Loren tidied away the plates when they were finished.

"We need to have another conversation, Nate."

Not meeting his gaze, Nathan nodded. "I know, Daddy. I'm sorry—"

"Wait. Let's get comfortable on the sofa first. I'm not sure how long this will take, and I don't want you getting sore or cold." Holding out his hand, Loren waited patiently for Nathan to decide if he wanted the support or not. Closing his eyes briefly when Nathan grabbed on, Loren led him to the sofa, snuggling Nathan into his body to keep him close. He knew they would need to be face to face for some of the conversation, but for the moment, Nathan was right where Loren needed him.

"Okay. What were you going to say in the kitchen?"

"I'm sorry about not leaving a note yesterday. It was after I spoke to Robbie that I realised I hadn't thought you might get home earlier than you said." Nathan glanced up at him.

Loren contemplated his answer. "Were you upset because you'd been out without telling me, or were you upset because you didn't want me to know?" The distinction was small but significant.

"Oh god, no! I didn't care if you knew I'd been out. I was upset because I didn't tell you." Nathan's gaze slid away from his. "There may have been another reason."

"Which is?" Loren had a feeling he knew what bothered Nathan, but he waited to see if his hunch was correct.

"I think I wanted to be punished," he muttered.

Loren's mouth curled up. Yeah, exactly what he thought. "You did it on purpose?"

"No, not consciously. Not at first, anyway." Nathan fiddled with the fabric of Loren's t-shirt.

"What do you mean, not at first?"

"Well, I left the house thinking I'd be back before you finished your work, so it didn't matter if I left a note or not. But when I spoke to Robbie, he told me I'd be punished for not telling you. By that point…" Nathan paused, then continued in a whisper, "I thought I may as well stay longer if I was going to get punished anyway."

Loren rolled his lips inwards to stop the smile spreading across his mouth. When he'd gained control, he replied, "I'm glad you told me. You will be punished, and you will not enjoy it, but you will also remember not to do it again. But after we have finished our conversation."

CHAPTER ELEVEN

NATHAN

Nathan was devastated when he found Loren curled up on the bedroom floor, something he never thought he'd see. And the way Loren had held him when he realised Nathan was there, it about broke his heart. If nothing else got through to him about how he felt about Loren…that did. He was falling hard for his Daddy. Telling him the truth about his thoughts had been difficult, but he felt better for it, although he was unsure about the rest of the conversation.

"What else do we need to talk about?"

Loren shifted, and Nathan sat up, facing him. "I'm going to put everything out there, Nathan. And you need to think about it and decide if you can put up with me as I am."

Gaze roaming the face of the man who had made Nathan feel complete for the first time, Nathan nodded.

"I need to care for a boy. I have to be in control of a lot of things most people wouldn't need to be in control of. I would like to help my boy to wash and dress, prepare his food, know where he is at all times, give him time to destress from his day-to-day issues, love him, care for him, punish him when he needs it." Loren cupped Nathan's jaw, gazing intently into his eyes. "I want to help him become the best version of himself he can be."

Unexpectedly, tears welled in Nathan's eyes and slid down his cheeks. Loren wiped them off.

"What's wrong, Nathan?"

Swallowing against the lump in his throat, Nathan decided to be honest, "I'd love that, too. I want to become the best I can be."

Loren beamed. "And you shall." He leaned forward, pulling Nathan towards him and pressed their lips together. "I will help you if you'll allow it."

"I'd love your help," he whispered.

Wrapping him in his arms, Loren pulled them back to their original position. "Nathan?"

"Yes, Daddy?"

"Will you stay here with me? I know it's quick, but I don't like the idea of you living on the streets when there is a place here for you."

Overwhelmed by the generosity, Nathan wanted to grab with both hands, but he was unsure if it was the right thing to do. "I'd love to, but…" He trailed off, not knowing how to explain his reservations.

"But, what, sweetheart?" Loren brushed his fingers through Nathan's hair.

"I don't want to take advantage of what you have here. I don't have a job, so won't be able to contribute to the bills. I can't cook, so can't help with it. I could clean but have never had to." Nathan felt like a failure in life.

"Nathan, look at me." Loren's voice brooked no argument. "You don't *have* to do anything. But," he continued when he saw Nathan was going to interrupt, "if you want to work, I can help you. What would you like to do?"

Nathan blinked at him. He hadn't thought about what he'd wanted to do for many years. He'd always thought about the things he would be *able* to do rather than what he *wanted* to do. Back when he was a teenager living at home, he had been good at school, and he'd wanted to do something to keep him interested. The only subject had been was mathematics. He'd planned on going to college in a mathematical field and seeing what jobs came up. But when he got kicked out, college went out of the window.

"I like maths, although I haven't done anything with it for years, it was something that interested me at school. I can add in my head quickly. I did it a lot when I went shopping for food to make sure I didn't go over what money I had."

"Budgeting, that's good. Anything else?"

"I didn't have any huge issues with schoolwork, but maths always held my attention." Loren chuckled. "What?"

"A man after my own heart."

Nathan snorted, realising, stupidly, Loren was right,

being an accountant dealt with a lot of maths. "Yeah. I never thought about it before."

They were quiet for a moment, then Loren started talking, "If maths is what you're interested in, I can teach you what I know. You can see whether accounting is something you might enjoy. If not, we can search for other job opportunities and see what is needed for them. You have a lot of options open to you, Nate, and I will be more than happy to help you if you want me to."

Nathan felt the prick of tears again but pushed it back. He crawled into Loren's lap, straddling his lap and burrowing his head into Loren's neck. "I'd love that," he whispered against his skin.

Loren rubbed a hand up and down his spine. "Would you like to stay?"

Nathan held him tighter. "Yes, please, Daddy." He felt a whoosh of air leave Loren's body, and Loren's arms coming around him to hold him as tightly as he held Loren.

"Thank you," Loren mumbled.

They stayed wrapped together for a while, and Nathan could feel himself becoming sleepy again, until Loren patted his ass.

"Time for your punishment, boy."

Nathan tensed but pulled away, resigned to his fate. "Yes, Daddy."

"Stand up." Nathan did reluctantly and watched as Loren moved to an armchair. "Joggers off and lay over my lap."

Nathan swallowed, briefly hesitated, then dropped

his joggers and trailed over. He leaned his stomach on Loren's thighs, his head and arms down.

"Move up a bit." Nathan was shifted into position by warm, strong hands, his head closer to the ground, his ass higher in the air. Not the most comfortable of positions, but that was the point. Loren smoothed a hand over his ass, and Nathan arched against him. "No moving. Your punishment is ten smacks. They will not be pleasant. They will hurt, but you will learn your lesson. And next time, we can do this for fun instead. Understand?"

"Yes, Daddy," Nathan replied with a tremor in his voice.

"Good." Loren slid his hand across his skin again. The heat left briefly. A sharp pain spread from the base of his ass outwards as Loren's palm connected. No soothing this time. Nine rapid successive smacks were administered, bringing tears to Nathan's eyes, but once the tenth was finished, a hand soothed his skin once more. "Well done, sweet boy. Well done."

Loren assisted Nathan to rise, the blood rushing from his head, making him dizzy. He stumbled, and Loren helped him lie on the sofa. Once he was settled, Loren disappeared for a moment, returning with a drink.

"Drink this." Loren took it from him once he'd finished and brushed his fingers through Nathan's hair again. "You did so well, Nathan. You're such a good boy for me."

Pleasure spread through Nathan's system; he had pleased his Daddy. "Thank you, Daddy."

"Rest there for a bit while I clean the kitchen." Loren pressed a kiss to Nathan's lips and drifted away.

Despite the sting in his ass, Nathan was relaxed and content, a feeling he hadn't felt for a long time.

He awoke warm and sleepy. A blanket was spread over him, and although he was naked from the waist down beneath it, he was toasty. He kept his eyes closed, relaxed as he was, but listened for sounds around him. There were repeated tapping and clicking noises which he eventually identified as typing and mouse buttons, and it came from the direction of the kitchen. He assumed Loren was working. Nathan blinked open his eyes, not wanting to emerge from his sleepy cocoon.

He snuggled deeper, wincing when his ass protested but smiling all the same. When his bladder wouldn't hold any longer, he untangled himself, standing immediately to not put pressure on his no doubt red ass and pulled on his joggers to visit the downstairs bathroom.

Studying himself in the mirror as he washed his hands, Nathan saw a brightness to his eyes he hadn't seen for a while, and he had Loren to thank for it. Thinking of Loren had Nathan seeking him out.

"Hello, Nate. Did you have a nice sleep?" Loren's gaze met his as he stopped his work.

"Yes, thank you, Daddy. Sorry. I didn't mean to sleep."

"It's okay, Nate. You needed the rest." Loren stood, coming towards him and pressing a kiss to his forehead. "Are you hungry?"

"A little."

"Okay." He returned to the table, picking up some

paper and placing it in Nathan's hands. "Sit and read this while I make us a snack." He veered Nathan towards a chair next to where he'd been sitting.

Frowning, Nathan studied the paper. It was an offer of an apprenticeship working for March Accountants. Nathan couldn't believe it. "What…?" He glanced over at Loren, who peered over his shoulder with a smile.

"You don't have to accept it, but I spoke to an acquaintance of mine. They have been searching for people to learn accounting from the beginning in the hopes those employees will stay with the company afterwards. They are a good company."

Nathan read over the offer again. He'd get minimal pay, naturally, but he would be taught everything there was to know about accounting. His breathing increased as he bit his lip, withholding the grin wanting to escape. "Why do they want me?"

"I put in a good word. I explained you didn't have any qualifications, but I would vouch for you." Loren shrugged as if it was no big deal.

"Why?" Nathan didn't understand why Loren would vouch for him when Loren had no idea what Nathan was capable of.

Loren turned and rested back against the counter, crossing his arms over his chest. "Because I know you'll work hard. And I believe if you begin to struggle, you will ask for help." He paused. "Am I wrong?"

"No!" Nathan shook his head vehemently. "I will work hard. I…Wow. Thank you."

Loren nodded in acknowledgement of the thanks.

"Do you want to know the best part? Or at least, I think it's the best part."

"What?"

"I'm the one training you."

The wealth of emotion was too much for Nathan to hold in at that point, and he burst into tears. He felt Loren's arms come around him, then he was lifted from the chair and settled into Loren's lap. He gripped the shirt below him, pressing his face into Loren's neck as the tears escaped. All he'd ever wanted was the opportunity to try and become something. Nathan had applied for hundreds of jobs over the last eleven years to no avail because they didn't want to take a chance on someone who was homeless. He was overwhelmed by the changes happening so quickly from a chance meeting in a dark alley.

He knew he would never be able to repay Loren for what he had given Nathan: a chance at a better life with someone who cared enough to help him.

Nathan took a cleansing breath, exhaling roughly but less shaky than the earlier one. Pulling back from Loren, he cupped his Daddy's jaw. "Thank you. From the bottom of my heart, thank you."

"You are welcome, Nathan."

Nathan became aware of the sting in his ass the longer he sat on Loren's lap. Wriggling to get more comfortable, he felt a chuckle run through Loren's chest.

"Are you uncomfortable, by any chance?"

"Yes, Daddy," Nathan whispered.

"Okay, let's stand. I can finish getting your snack ready."

Nathan followed him into the kitchen and washed his hands, ready to eat.

"Here we are." Loren passed a plate to him filled with melon slices, orange segments, apple slices and a little pot of yoghurt in the middle. "This should fill you up until lunchtime."

"Thank you, Daddy." Nathan rested back, making sure his lower back touched the edge of the counter but not his ass, and proceeded to eat. Out the corner of his eye, he could see Loren watching him over a cup of coffee. He wasn't sure what the perusal was about, but he enjoyed being the focus of his attention.

When Nathan had cleared the plate, Loren took it from his hands, rinsed it off and stacked it in the dishwasher. Loren stood in front of Nathan, lifting his chin.

"Are you okay with everything that has happened over the last few days? It's a lot to take in, I know. But I need to know if you're okay with it all."

Nathan rested his palms against Loren's chest, running them up and down the fabric as he watched. He thought through everything that had happened since the incident in the alley. "I am fine with it." He met Loren's troubled gaze. "It's a bit of an adjustment after eleven years, but I am coping. You are being amazingly patient with me, and I love it." *I love you.* Nathan dropped his gaze, biting his lip to stop the words from escaping. They weren't there yet, but Nathan realised how true his feelings were.

Loren was a good man and an amazing Daddy. He

took care of Nathan, always making sure he had what he needed and helped him to figure out what he wanted for the rest of his life. And trying to make it happen.

Nathan's body filled with emotion, and he felt light as air. Nobody had ever made him feel like this.

Loren lifted his chin once more and pressed their lips together in a sweet meeting, kissing his top lip, then his bottom lip and sipping from his mouth before pulling away.

"I have some more work to do. Why don't you go have a bath? Soak your behind a little," he said with a smirk.

"Yes, Daddy." Nathan felt his cheeks heat.

Loren snickered, kissed him once more and let him go.

Nathan drifted to the en-suite, set the bath running and stood, staring at his reflection. His life had changed dramatically in the last few days, but Robbie and Daisy's had, too. He needed to speak to Loren about what he could do to help them, especially with their baby on the way. He knew Daisy had said there was time, but life on the streets was hard for adults. For children or adults with babies, it was terrible. He needed to figure out his options.

The apprenticeship Loren had secured was an amazing start at getting where he wanted to be—a valuable member of the relationship and a working person—but he wanted to help more homeless people. He didn't know if his maths could help, but they could think of something together.

Together.

That was another thing. He now had someone to care about what happened to him. Don't get him wrong, Robbie and Daisy would've cared, but they had each other. It was slightly different.

His brain went round and round in circles, so he stepped into the bathwater and gingerly sat, hissing at the temperature when it hit his ass. Once he was settled, he rested his head back and relaxed. His body, including his ass, soon got used to the heat, and his limbs turned heavy. He couldn't believe how much he'd slept today already, but he could easily sleep again.

Returning his thoughts to Loren, Nathan smiled. He'd been searching for a Daddy for a long time, and a chance encounter found him one perfect for him.

EIGHT MONTHS LATER

LOREN

Loren dreamed of the tongue-lashing Nathan had given him the previous day, the wet heat surrounding his cock as he thrust into Nathan's throat. He couldn't think; he could only act. Reaching down, he gripped the light brown strands, watching the red tinges appear in the slight glow of the light.

As his orgasm came to fruition, he awoke, opening his eyes and locking gazes with the beautiful chestnut-brown eyes of his boy. The muscles in his torso clenched in time with his climax, but he couldn't pull his gaze away as Nathan swallowed everything his Daddy gave him. When his brain had calmed, and his breath had returned to normal, he narrowed his gaze at the naughty boy lying between his legs.

"You, boy, are in big trouble."

Nathan batted his eyelashes in a fake apology.

"Sorry, Daddy. You were aroused, and I couldn't resist."

"Uh-huh. Go have a shower, boy. Your guests will be arriving soon; therefore, your punishment will be doled out later." Loren gave him a small push, making Nathan jump off the bed, talking a mile a minute.

"I can't wait to see them. Robbie has done well with the job the shelter found him, and though he'd not been there for long, they gave him the paternity leave. He does have to go back in a couple of days, but it will be nice to see them again. I hope Daisy is getting some sleep. She looked terrible the last time I saw her. I told Robbie he needed to help out more because Daisy didn't seem well. Hopefully, he's..."

The dialogue continued as Nathan stepped into the shower, but Loren had no hope of hearing what was said.

How his boy had changed since they first met. Gone was the quiet, reserved boy who didn't want to impose, and in his place was a talkative, social butterfly. And Loren loved it. Their dynamic was pretty much the same as it had been from the start, except for Nathan pushing the boundaries a lot more.

Loren pulled on his boxers and padded over to the en-suite.

"...see about getting a house nearby or something. I said I'd speak to you because I have no idea about properties."

"Nathan."

Nathan stopped soaping his body and glanced over his shoulder. "Yes, Daddy."

"Breathe." Loren watched as Nathan's chest expanded and collapsed twice, nodding. "Better. I know you are excited about them visiting, but you need to calm down. When you've finished your shower, I will help you get dressed, and you can colour while I make breakfast."

Nathan closed his eyes briefly. "Thank you, Daddy."

Loren retraced his steps, heading for the drawers and pulling out a navy-blue t-shirt, black jeans, blue socks and underwear. When Loren had found out the blue was Nathan's favourite colour, he had purposefully bought several clothes in varying shades for him; it appeared to help him relax and be more confident. Laying them out on the bed, Loren pulled on his own clothes.

Exiting the bathroom in a cloud of steam, Nathan was naked as the day he was born, drying his hair with a towel. It wasn't as long as it had been but long enough for Loren to grab in his fist.

"Come here, sweet boy."

Nathan strode over after dropping the towel in the laundry basket. He stood in front of Loren, eyes and face smiling, limbs loose.

Picking up the underwear, Loren kneeled at Nathan's feet, holding them out for him to step into then slid them slowly up his legs. Goosebumps followed in his wake, earning a smirk from Loren. He tucked Nathan's semi-hard cock into the underwear, patting it gently as he finished and grabbed the trousers, repeating the process. As he fastened the button and zip, Loren could hear Nathan's rapid breathing and noticed his fists were clenched at his sides. Willing to have Nathan squirming for a while as part of his punishment, Loren helped him with his socks, each movement excruciatingly slow. Lastly, Loren stood with the t-shirt. Lifting Nathan's arms over his head, Loren pulled it down over his arms and covering his face. Before pulling it on, and while Nathan's face was covered, he leaned down and nibbled at both Nathan's nipples in turn, earning a growl in response. He tugged the material into place, revealing the pained gaze of his boy.

"Time for breakfast."

"Daddy!"

"Come on, sweet boy. Let's go." Loren led the way out of the room and down the stairs. He rounded the counter, pulling out the colouring book and pencils and placing them in front of Nathan. "I think today is the day for pancakes and syrup. What do you think, Nate?"

Nathan did a little victory dance on the stool and pumped his arms in the air. "Yes, please, Daddy!"

Loren snorted and shook his head at Nathan's antics, inwardly over the moon at the response. As he prepared the batter mix, he glanced over at Nathan, occasionally smiling at the tip of his tongue peeking through his teeth as he concentrated on colouring. Although Nathan didn't regress to being a little, he enjoyed the mindless tasks, which helped his mind to settle and recuperate from everyday life.

By chance, Loren had found trains were something

Nathan liked, so they'd ended up with a toy train track and some accessories much to Nathan's delight. It wasn't a young boy's toy; it was for older children and had remote-controlled trains instead of push-along ones. Regardless of the age for the toy, Nathan loved it and often brought it out to watch the trains going round and round the track endlessly. On those days, Loren knew Nathan needed extra time to destress. It wasn't often Nathan needed the trains, but when he did, he'd had a busy day.

Flipping the final pancake onto the plate, Loren turned off the oven. "Time to tidy up, Nate."

"Okay, Daddy." Nathan began repacking the crayons straight away, and Loren knew he hadn't been in the zone. He was too excited to see his friends.

Placing a plate in front of Nathan when the table was clear, he dribbled some syrup over the top just as Nathan liked and watched him grin as the syrup ran down like lava.

"Thank you, Daddy."

"You're welcome."

They ate in silence, Nathan finishing his pile before Loren was halfway through. He didn't say anything. Out the corner of his eye, he watched Nathan fidget, his gaze bouncing around the room, and Loren withheld his smile as he continued eating.

When the doorbell rang, his eardrum was blasted by Nathan shouting, "They're here!" and running towards the front door. Loren snorted and shook his head, a regular occurrence for him.

Putting the plates in the sink, he heard multiple

voices and wandered down the hall to greet the visitors.

"Good morning, Robbie, Daisy. How are things?" Loren shook hands with Robbie and hugged Daisy, seeing she was indeed looking a lot healthier for this visit.

"Great, thanks, Loren," Robbie replied.

"Easy for you to say, Mr Heavy-Sleeper," Daisy raised one eyebrow in Robbie's direction, and Loren chuckled.

"Can I see my beautiful goddaughter?" Nathan asked, bouncing on his toes.

Daisy laughed. "Sure." She twisted the car seat around, revealing a tiny pink bundle fast asleep.

"She's so cute," Nathan whispered, kneeling next to baby Lexi on the floor.

"Nathan? Why don't we take her into the living room, and you can sit next to her on the rug? You'll be more comfortable there than on the hard floor," Loren advised.

"Okay, Daddy." Nathan jumped up from the floor, and, carefully, picked up the seat, trailing slowly towards the living room.

Loren smirked. Nathan had never been around babies and didn't understand their resilience. Every time he saw Lexi, he treated her like a china doll. Every movement he made was slow, careful and measured around her. He adored the eight-day-old baby.

Loren knew Nathan would make a great father one

day. And Loren wouldn't object to the idea either. But that was in the distant future, anyhow.

"Would you like something to drink?"

"A cup of tea would be nice, if it's not too much trouble?"

"Not at all, Daisy. Robbie?"

"Coffee if you have some, if not, tea is fine. Thanks, Loren." Robbie sat on the sofa next to Daisy and rested his head on the back. If anything, Robbie appeared more tired and Daisy less so.

The morning was spent in great company and with great conversation. Much to Nathan's unhappiness, his friends left in the early afternoon, citing the need for more sleep. Loren prepared a snack for Nathan, hoping to boost his mood, but he sat on the sofa, crossed legged, staring at the TV.

Loren knew how to take his mind off things.

"Nathan?" When he peered over at Loren, he continued, "Go to the bedroom and strip. Leave your clothes tidy and lay on the bed on your front."

Nathan's eyes widened, and he scrambled to do what Loren asked.

Grabbing a bottle from the cupboard in the kitchen, Loren followed at a more sedate pace, giving Nathan time to do as asked. When he entered the room, Nathan was in the perfect position. Loren wandered to the end of the bed and dropped the bottle on the cover. He stripped out of his clothes, folding them and placing them on the chair with Nathan's and crawled onto the bed, straddling Nathan's thighs.

Clicking open the bottle, he poured a little of the contents into his palm, sealed the bottle again and began rubbing his hands together. The lavender oil warmed, and he placed his hands on Nathan's back. Rubbing in long movements up and down his spine, he made sure every expanse of skin was covered, sometimes rubbing firm, sometimes soft.

Loren's cock was hard, and he purposefully teased Nathan's crack every time he pushed his hands to Nathan's shoulders, then pulled away when he lowered them. The moans, groans and pleas falling from Nathan's lips made Loren leer. Punishment could be enacted in different ways.

Bucking his hips into the mattress below, Nathan pleaded for relief, but Loren refused, even when Loren's hands descended to massage Nathan's ass cheeks and upper thighs.

"Please, Daddy."

Deciding to give Nathan some relief, but only minor, Loren told him he could turn over.

"Thank you, Daddy."

Loren smirked. He filled his palm again and proceeded to repeat the whole process on the front of Nathan's body, this time Loren's cock pressed against Nathan's cock, making Nathan bite his lip. No doubt withholding the curses he wanted to say.

When Nathan's body trembled so hard, he was practically vibrating and his cock streamed precome, Loren felt his control falter. He turned Nathan onto his front once more, lifting him to his knees, and prepared him. Loren knew Nathan enjoyed a small bite of pain with the initial entry. He used two fingers then lubed his shaft, leaning over his back.

"Mine!" Loren called as he breached Nathan's hole.

"Yes, Daddy! Yours! Always yours!" Nathan braced himself on his hands, pushing back against Loren.

Thrusting his hips in a punishing rhythm, Loren lost himself to the feeling of Nathan. One hand gripped Nathan's hip, the other his shoulder, giving him more leverage. His orgasm was fast approaching, he canted his hips slightly, knowing the correct angle and was rewarded with a cry of release. The vice clenching his cock brought his climax forward, and he shouted Nathan's name.

When their legs could no longer hold them up, they cuddled up with Nathan's back to Loren's chest, regaining their breath.

"I love you, Daddy."

"I love you, sweet boy."

Would you like the next book in the series? Soothe Me, Daddy, Book 2 follows Isaac and Henley as they figure out how to balance their Daddy/boy relationship with working together.

Sign up to my newsletter to get a free Crush prequel short story, Love Conquers and a serial newsletter story every month.

If you have a moment, would you write a review

for Love Me, Daddy please? Reviews help other readers decide whether they would like to read the book, and therefore, are also important for authors.

130

ABOUT ELOUISE EAST

I am Elouise East but feel free to call me Elli. I write sweet and steamy connections in gay romance. I also touch on taboo stories under the name Elouise R East.

Books that tell the stories where friendship and family are the focal point - be it blood family or chosen - is very important to me. That's why I include a variety of personalities, talents, ages, situations and abilities as I believe a story needs, or a character needs. I want my characters to be real, to be relatable, to be free to have whatever views they tell me they have. And trust me, most of the time, I do not have *any* say in the matter!

My characters come to life on the page for me as well as my readers. Their stories unfold in front of me, and I have very little input into how they want to be shown. Just like real life, the lives of my characters change with every choice, every interaction and every conversation. And I wouldn't have it any other way.

I write books that are emotionally realistic, even if liberties are taken with other aspects of my stories. I don't know any other way to write. It comes from deep inside.

Who am I? A single parent to two children who

make life worth living. An avid reader who still devours every book she can get her hands on. A student of learning about any subject that takes her fancy. An author of books she would read herself. And a romantic at heart who loves anything cheesy.

Who's in?

←――――――――――――――――→

Stalk me here… ;-)
https://elouiseeast.com/
https://elouiseeast.com/newsletter
https://linktr.ee/elouiseeastauthor

Check out https://elouiseeast.com/books for my books!

BOOKS BY ELOUISE EAST

<u>DADDY</u>

Love Me, Daddy

Soothe Me, Daddy

Spoil Me, Daddy

<u>CRUSH</u>

First Kiss

Instant Desire

Primary Seduction

Deep Down

A Crush for Christmas

Life Support

Covert Strength

Love Scene

Lawful Attraction

CLUB ROYAL

Royal Firsts

Rogue Royal

Secretive Royal

Grieving Royal

Disowned Royal

Trained Royal

Awakened Royal

Commanding Royal

LOVE IN FLAMES

Out of the Frying Pan

Smokescreen

Breathing Fire

JUST A LITTLE CRUSH

Star-Crossed

He's Behind You

A Special Love (newsletter story)

DARK & DIVERGENT

A Biker Make Three

Forbidden Temptation

Too Many Secrets

<u>STANDALONE</u>

Treehouse Whispers